A note on the author

Denzil Meyrick was born in Glasgow and brought up in Campbeltown. After studying politics, he pursued a varied career including time spent as a police officer, freelance journalist and director of several companies in the leisure, engineering and marketing sectors. Denzil lives on Loch Lomond side with his wife, Fiona.

Also by Denzil Meyrick

D.C.I. Daley thriller series

Whisky from Small Glasses
The Last Witness
Dark Suits and Sad Songs
The Rat Stone Serenade
Well of the Winds
The Relentless Tide
A Breath on Dying Embers
Jeremiah's Bell
For Any Other Truth
The Death of Remembrance

Tales from Kinloch

A Large Measure of Snow
A Toast to the Old Stones

Short Stories

One Last Dram Before Midnight

Terms of Restitution

GHOSTS IN THE GLOAMING

A TALE FROM KINLOCH

Denzil Meyrick

Polygon

First published in Great Britain in 2022 by Polygon, an imprint of Birlinn Ltd.

Birlinn Ltd
West Newington House
10 Newington Road
Edinburgh
EH9 1QS

www.polygonbooks.co.uk

1

ISBN 978 1 84697 615 5
eBook ISBN 978 1 78885 555 6

British Library Cataloguing-in-Publication Data
A catalogue record for this book is available on request from the British Library.

Typeset by Initial Typesetting Services, Edinburgh

In memory of every soul who set sail never to return.

*Every new beginning comes from
some other beginning's end.*

Seneca

PROLOGUE

Kinloch, June 1920

The morning had dawned bright and warm. After the unremitting hell of the war years, the place was finally getting back to the old, much-loved traditions, resurrected and ready to be enjoyed by the good folk of the town.

Young Sandy Hoynes, flushed with success following his successful navigation exam at the Ministry of Agriculture and Fisheries, stood on the pier. He couldn't wait for the fancy certificate to arrive, so that he could frame it on the living-room wall at his parents' home. A pair of stout oars were cradled in the crook of his right arm. The sun shone on his golden hair, as the summer breeze tugged a strand across his tanned face. For the sixteen-year-old boy life was good – very good. He took in the scene before him through blue, blue eyes, smiling benignly at all around.

It was nearly midday, and hundreds of grinning, laughing, happy people thronged the harbour, awaiting the fun and frolics the day was sure to provide. For Kinloch stayed true to its seafaring traditions. Elsewhere, there were Highland games, with hammer throwing, caber tossing, tug o' war and the like. But this community enjoyed its sport on the blue waters of the loch. For them, there was no challenge like a maritime one. The air was heavy with the smell of beer, whisky and tobacco smoke, and the enticing aroma of sweetmeats being sold from stalls drifted along the promenade. After such dark days, and so many lost souls, this was akin to rebirth.

'That tub won't make it to the island and back,' said a dour-faced lad. He nodded to the rowing boat that Sandy and his father had built with such love, care and pride over the last two years.

'Your backside, Dreich MacCallum,' Sandy replied, eyeing his critic with a flashing dislike. Though the lad – a year older than Sandy – stood tall, he was painfully thin. He was known to everyone as 'Dreich', after the good old Scots word for grey, rainy, miserable weather, and suited the moniker perfectly. He had little to say that wasn't fault-finding or dismissive of others, and Sandy couldn't remember ever seeing him smile.

'My faither says that you and your old man can't mend a net, never mind build a boat,' Dreich continued.

'Does he now? But you think that leaky old sieve of yours will stay afloat until we're out of the harbour? Man, it looks as though it's leaning to port, as it is,' said Sandy. Sure enough, the venerable rowing boat that Dreich MacCallum was to use in the race to the island and back appeared to have a distinct list to starboard.

'I'll bet you tuppence it does!'

'You're on.' Sandy spat on his hand, and the pair shook on it. 'Mind you, if you do win, it'll be consolation for failing your navigation exam – again.' Sandy grinned at Dreich, taking him in from the corner of his eye.

'I did not fail!'

'Auld Watson the clerk said you did. He told my father.

Man, they were having a right good laugh aboot it at the Douglas Arms just last night, apparently. You'll be thirty before you pass, so they're saying.'

It was true to say there were challenges surrounding the award of a navigation certificate in Kinloch. Only five such qualifications were handed out per year, based on the top papers returned. It was also true to say that, if one was fortunate enough to sit the exam during a dearth of sufficiently bright mariners, the chances of being successful rose exponentially. But that was just the way it was.

Dreich furrowed his brow, a wicked sneer playing across his lips. 'Och, we'll just need to wait and see, Sandy Hoynes. I hear the certificates will be out soon.'

Just as Sandy was about to reply with a witty remark, a whistle blew, and the competitors were called to their positions. The rules were simple: when the starting pistol sounded, each lad, oars in hand, had to race down the steps at the corner of the harbour, get into their rowing boat, and set off. The winner would be the first oarsman who managed to round the buoy near the island at the head of the loch and make it back across the finishing line, a notional one between Kinloch's two piers.

'Good luck to you all!' shouted harbour master Johnson. He hefted the starting pistol in the air. There followed a tantalising wait before a sharp report sounded, the crowd cheered, and ten young men pelted down the slick steps, then waded out to their boats.

Young Billy Duncan was unlucky straight away. He took a tumble and emerged from the still waters of the loch with a bloody gash to his right elbow. The rest, however, made it safely into their boats, and with much plunging of oars, jostling, and one or two oaths, set off like a small flotilla in the foaming water.

Beyond the protective arms of the harbour, the going became more troublesome. The sea was choppy despite the light breeze. The churning produced by so many sets of oars working away in such close proximity ensured that each young man must pay close attention, lest a collision occur. This wasn't just a battle of strength but one of skill, judgement and seamanship.

Two leaders emerged. Sandy Hoynes and Dreich MacCallum were neck and neck as they neared the buoy, placed just before the causeway to the island. Not far away, a fishing boat bobbed with two umpires aboard, there to make sure each craft followed the rules and no corners were cut.

Sandy was narrowly in the lead as he and Dreich turned towards the buoy in order to navigate their way around it. But young Sandy was unlucky; a rogue wave caught him amidships just as he executed his turn. His rowing boat wallowed alarmingly, drifting away from the obstacle and allowing Dreich to cut inside to the shorter line.

Undaunted, Sandy bent his back into the oars and pushed on. In a few seconds, the boats were level again.

'You'll be down tuppence!' shouted Sandy as he looked across at Dreich's boat. The rest of the field were only just rounding the buoy, carefully scrutinised by the umpires.

Without warning, Dreich angled his little rowing boat to port, and headed straight for Sandy. Though the latter tried his best to avoid it, their oars entwined. Before he knew it, and with surprising strength considering his slender frame, Dreich caught Sandy by surprise. He wound his oar a few times like someone churning butter, and thrust his competitor's oar into the air. Sandy felt it slip from his hands, and despite his best efforts he lost his grip. The oar slid through the rowlock and, propelled by the churned-up water between the pair, drifted away from the boat.

'I'll be waiting for you on the pier. Be ready wae your money!' shouted Dreich, working hard and pulling away from the stricken Sandy.

Forced to pursue his lost oar, Sandy looked on with dismay as the rest of the field sailed past him. By the time he managed to retrieve it, Sandy was in last place, with no chance of winning. Though he managed to pass a couple of stragglers, by the time he reached the finishing line, Dreich was being cheered to the echo as he mounted the steps and set foot back on dry land, arms aloft in triumph.

Sandy's father was standing at the top of the steps as his son secured his boat and struggled back onto the pier. He was holding a piece of paper in one hand, a grim look on his face.

'Did she no' sail well, Sandy?'

'No, she sailed just fine. Dreich caught my oar with his, and it ended up in the water.'

'Aye, such things can happen in a close contest. There's always next year, son.'

'He did it on purpose, Faither. He's a bloody cheat!'

'Now, you watch your language, Alexander.' His father only used his proper name when his son had done something wrong.

Back on the pier, Sandy apologised. The race run, crowds now thronged the stalls, so they were on their own at the steps. Sandy looked at the paper his father held in his great paw. There was something odd about him, a shuffling from foot to foot. Sandy had rarely seen him look awkward – nervous, even.

'Is there something the matter, Faither? Apart fae losing the race, I mean.'

The big man handed his son the paper. It was a letter from the Ministry of Agriculture and Fisheries.

'My certificate!' Sandy grabbed the letter and unfolded it.

Dear Master Hoynes,

I regret to inform that you failed to reach the standard required to award our Standard Navigation Certificate. I enclose an application form for next year's exam, should it be required.

Yours sincerely,
Thos. MacFarlane
Senior Clerk

Sandy read the letter again, just in case he'd misunderstood. But on second inspection – if anything – the words appeared even starker than before.

'I'm sorry, son. We'll get into the books before you sit it again next year.'

'But auld Wattie told you I'd passed. He marked the paper, didn't he?'

'Aye, he did. Och, he must have got it wrong, Sandy. It's fair to say he'd had a drink or two when he imparted that information to me, right enough.' Sandy's father cleared his throat. 'Anyway, I better get back to your mother before she buys any more tat from these stalls.' He smiled at his son. 'Try not to be too disappointed, Sandy. What's for you won't go by you. Remember that.' He walked back to the promenade and soon vanished into the crowd.

Despite his father's encouragement, though, Sandy couldn't help feeling utterly miserable. He'd been cheated out of the race and, worse still, had failed his navigation exam. The day just couldn't get worse, as far as he was concerned.

Sandy felt a tap on his shoulder. 'Dreich, if you've come for your tuppence, you'll have to wait. My money's at home. I'll give it to you this afternoon.' He paused. 'Even though you cheated.'

The reply surprised him.

'Take your time. I'll no' have time to get the money from you this afternoon. My faither's taking us out for high tea at the County Hotel.'

'Wonderful. Have a great time.'

Dreich delved into the pocket of his short trousers and produced a folded piece of paper. 'You see, we're celebrating.' He waved the letter in Sandy's face. 'This is from the Ministry. I passed my exam after all.'

'Eh?'

'Aye, no more worries about navigation for me.' He looked slyly at the younger man. 'Of course, you'll have yours, too. Are you away out for high tea?'

Sandy bunched his fist. 'I don't know how you did it, Dreich. But you know as well as I do you failed that paper.'

Dreich, perhaps for the first time in his life, smiled broadly. He took a step towards Sandy and lowered his voice. 'Of course I did. But my faither's great friends with the Fisheries Officer. Do you understand?'

Sandy was aghast. 'I understand you're a liar and a cheat, Dreich MacCallum!'

'It's sad. But someone had to miss out this year. There can only be five passes, you know.'

Still brooding on his disappointments, Sandy hadn't fully taken in what Dreich had said. But now the truth dawned on him. Not only had he been cheated out of the race, he'd also been cheated out of his navigation certificate. Without thought, Sandy tightened his balled fist and swung it into the face of his tormentor.

1

Kinloch, December 1968

Though the weather was miserable, at least there was no sign of the blizzards that Kinloch had encountered in the lead-up to the previous year's festive season. Just the same, Hamish huddled into his pea jacket against the cold, while clamping his Breton cap on his head to prevent the strong wind from carrying it off. He shivered as he turned into Sandy Hoynes's street. The scheme sat on a hill overlooking the town, a bracing five-minute walk in good weather but a real trudge in conditions like this.

But Hamish was answering a call for help and felt duty-bound to answer that call.

He plodded along the street just as the rain began to pelt down. He stopped, pushed at the garden gate, and was soon on the steps of number 76, where he knocked on the door and waited. Sure enough, a light appeared behind the frosted glass, and a figure could be seen making its way down the hall.

'Hamish, you're a sight for sore eyes,' said Marjorie Hoynes. She was pulling a long Aran cardigan close to her ample frame in order to keep out the cold. 'It's a terrible night. Come in, lad.'

Hamish wiped his feet on the doormat and stepped into the Hoynes's hallway.

'Come and get a heat at the fire,' said Mrs Hoynes, ushering the young fisherman into the cosy living room. The place was neat and tidy, with a fine fire in the hearth and an artificial Christmas tree standing on the sideboard. Festive cards were dotted about the place, some on a string above the fireplace. 'You take Sandy's seat beside the hearth, Hamish. Get yourself warmed up. Can I get you a cup of tea – a dram, maybe?'

Though Hamish was sorely tempted to accept the offer of a restorative whisky, he opted for tea for politeness's sake. He watched the flames dance in the grate, warming his hands against it, as Mrs Hoynes went about the business of making tea.

She returned to the room with a tray, on which sat two cups and saucers, a plate of shortbread, a red teapot, sugar bowl and small jug of milk.

'You take sugar, don't you?'

'Aye, three spoons, if you don't mind, Mrs Hoynes.'

'You're nearly as bad as Sandy wae his sweet tooth.'

'He takes four. Many a cup of tea I've made him, right enough. He says the stuff's pure poison wae no sugar on board, so to speak.'

'Aye, that sounds like oor Sandy.' Mrs Hoynes poured Hamish's tea, added a drop of milk and three spoons of sugar. She handed it to him. 'Help yourself to shortbread, Hamish. I made it today.'

Remembering how tasty Mrs Hoynes's shortbread was, Hamish was tempted to take two pieces, but decency forced his hand and he only availed himself of the one.

'You'll have had a lean time, what wae the boat up on

Galbraith's slip,' said Mrs Hoynes. The *Girl Maggie* had been out of the water for three weeks because of a problem with her Gardiner engine. The wait was on for a part from Glasgow. It was of such a specific nature that one day had rolled into another, and still there was no sign.

'Aye, the days have been quite long. But it's nice to have a wee holiday,' said Hamish.

'And Christmas and the New Year will tide you over. I'm sure the boat will be back in the water by the first week in January.'

It was only now that Hamish noticed how worn-out she looked. Mrs Hoynes's face was pale and there were large bags under her eyes she'd done her best to hide with powder.

'How is he today?'

'Och, Hamish. I've never seen Sandy like this. Not in all the years I've been married to him. It's like living with a stranger, so it is. He's just fair scunnered at everything. I took him a plate o' mince earlier – didna eat half o' it.'

'And he fair likes his mince and tatties.'

'There's no' a body that enjoys them more.'

'Is he taking a refreshment?'

'Whisky?'

Hamish nodded.

'He's no' touched a drop since he arrived back from the County that night. Och, it must be near enough two weeks ago.'

Hamish frowned. Mince and tatties were one thing, but whisky was another matter altogether. The man he knew enjoyed a moderate drink every day – sometimes not that moderate. To have been two weeks without a drop was surely some kind of record.

'We should maybe call the Guinness people. You know, them wae the book,' said Hamish, by way of lightening the mood.

Mrs Hoynes looked confused. 'If he'll no' take a dram, I doubt he'll want a pint o' Guinness. He's never been that fond of the stuff, Hamish.' She shook her head. 'Can I ask you, did anything happen that night? Anything untoward, I mean.'

Hamish had pondered this himself. Though, if he was honest, that particular evening was quite disjointed in his memory.

'We'd a good night, Mrs H. Sandy seemed full o' the joys. An old friend of his arrived in the County. Man, they were fair reminiscing, the pair o' them. Och, the drams were flying. You know how it is.'

Hamish looked on as his host's face changed. Suddenly Mrs Hoynes's expression altered from one of concern to downright panic.

'We didna have too many drams. I'm sure Sandy had only maybe three or four,' said Hamish, wishing he'd kept quiet on the subject of alcohol.

'This friend. Can you remember his name?'

The young fisherman's mind was a blank. Hamish had never been good at names, and faced with a crisis, the likelihood of him remembering someone he'd only met once in a haze of whisky was remote.

'You know, I canna, Mrs H. I get fair confused with names. I just canna mind, at all.'

'Did this man have a nickname?'

Ah, now that did ring a bell. He racked his brain, desperately trying to remember what it was. He was convinced that the nickname was an unusual one. But still it wouldn't come.

'Could it have been Dreich, by any chance?' said Mrs Hoynes.

Hamish pulled off his cap, revealing his alarmingly retreating hairline. 'Man, you've got it! That's just who the gentleman was. If I have it right, he's in Kinloch until the middle of January. He's a sea captain on one of these luxury cruise liners. You know, like the *Queen Mary* – though it canna be her as she's retired.'

'Oh, goodness me.' Mrs Hoynes worked a handkerchief between her hands.

'Do you no' like this Dreich fella, Mrs H?'

'I can barely remember him, if I'm honest. But if there's one man in the world who Sandy despises, it's Dreich MacCallum.'

'Aye, that's it! Dreich MacCallum. A right odd nickname, if you ask me. He's got a good pouring arm, mind – very generous. I canna think why the skipper dislikes him so much. They seemed to be getting on like a house on fire, and that's a fact.'

'It's a long story, Hamish. Oh, I know Sandy wouldn't let on in public. But there's bad blood between those two that goes back decades. That's what Sandy says, at least. He mentions him now and again, but mostly when he's drunk or in a bad mood. Though he's never once said what happened.'

Hamish frowned. 'This Dreich bloke wisna the one who borrowed all that money then ran off to Australia, was it?'

Mrs Hoynes shook her head. 'No, that was Scunner Boyd.'

'Right. What about the swine who sold him the stolen car?'

'Doddie McGarry.'

'Oh aye. I remember the name now.' Hamish sighed. 'Do

you mind the time he was reported for being drunk in charge of his bike? Man, he wasn't pleased about that at all.'

'No, it all goes back long before any of that, Hamish.' Mrs Hoynes shook her head and dabbed a tear from her eye. 'Would you mind taking the stairs and having a word with him?'

'Of course.'

'You're a good lad – a credit to your mother, right enough. How is she, by the way?'

Hamish sighed. 'Just the same, Mrs H. We're off to her cousin Mary's for Christmas dinner this year. I'm sure my mother's no' happy aboot it.'

'All this fuss. When I was a girl, folk used to go to the church on Christmas Day, if they had a mind. But it was a day like most others. We had our presents at New Year, such as they were. I can see a day coming when Hogmanay will be a thing of the past, the way things are going.'

'No first footing? No, that'll never happen. It's the best bit o' the holiday. Folk getting together to celebrate another year. That'll last for ever.'

Mrs Hoynes shrugged. 'Would you like to go up now, Hamish?'

'No bother. Will I take him some tea?'

'Aye, but he'll only take it in a certain way, as you know.'

Mrs Hoynes disappeared into the kitchen and returned holding a chipped enamel mug with a blue rim. 'I'm right embarrassed when anyone sees this. But you know fine what he's like.'

'Aye, he has one like it on the boat.'

'When we went for a trip to Edinburgh, he took it with him. There he was in the hotel dining room wae this damned thing. Folk were fair gawping at us.'

Mrs Hoynes poured tea into the old mug, added four heaped teaspoons of sugar, a splash of milk and stirred.

Mug in hand, Hamish ascended the stairs to see his ailing skipper.

2

Though the carpet on the stairs was thick, the wood underneath protested at Hamish's tread. He wasn't quite sure in which room he would find his skipper, but his first guess proved to be right. On opening the door at the end of the landing, he was greeted by a wall of tobacco smoke. Sandy Hoynes might have foresworn alcohol, but he hadn't set his pipe aside; that much was obvious.

The bedroom was in darkness, save for a chink of light coming through a gap in the curtains from the streetlamps outside. Hamish could hear the rain battering off the window and shuddered at the thought of facing the elements again on his way home.

'Who's that?' said Hoynes, his voice cracked and weak.

'It's me, Hamish. I've brought you some tea, skipper.'

Hoynes was just a dark huddle in the bed. 'Don't put that big light on – I'm no' decent.'

'Are you in the scud?' Hamish blanched at the thought.

'No, I've no' got my bunnet on. Wait till I find the bloody thing.'

Bunnet found, Hoynes struggled onto one side and switched on a small bedside light. Though this did illuminate the room to some extent, it was with a pale sepia glow.

Hoynes propped himself up on a cascade of pillows, his striped flannelette pyjama top just visible above the faded red of the candlewick bedspread, and adjusted his fisherman's cap over his tousled grey locks.

He was a sorry sight. For a start, Hamish had rarely seen his skipper out of his sea jumper. Only at weddings and funerals did Hoynes deign to wear anything else, and even then, it was under protest. And there was a bleakness about him; with the pale face and sunken eyes, he almost looked like a stranger.

'Here's your tea, Sandy.'

Hoynes took the mug and slurped at the beverage. 'Man, it's fair stewed! How long did it take you to get up those stairs?'

'It was fae the pot me and your good lady shared. I can go and get you a fresh one, if you like.'

'No, son. It's no' worth it. I think my tea-drinking days are coming to an end, and that's a fact.'

'Are you moving onto the coffee?'

'Hamish, you're no' a man for subtlety, are you?'

'How so?'

'For when a body declares their tea-drinking days to be over, it's an intimation that they're not long for this world.'

'Don't say that!'

'It's nothing but the truth. When you get to my age, you can feel yourself running down like an old engine out of oil. It's the way the Good Lord intended, and there's nothing to lament aboot – that's a fact.'

'I think it's a trip to the surgery you're needing, Sandy.'

'There's no doctor can save me. And anyway, you'll have heard about Dr McMurdo and his brother?'

'No, I canna say I have, to be honest.'

Hoynes cleared his throat and sat up in bed. 'You'll know that one brother – Kenny – is the doctor, and the other, his twin – Ross – is a lawyer?'

'Aye, I know the pair of them. Snooty buggers, if you ask me.'

'That aside, they've much to hide, I'll tell you.'

'Eh?'

'Kenny likes a refreshment, as you know. In fact, I think it's fair to say he's one of the most refreshed men I know.'

'Aye, he takes a good bucket, and that's for sure.'

Hoynes beckoned Hamish to come nearer to the bed. He lowered his voice. 'The tale I'm hearing is that, on a number of occasions recently, Kenny has been too far gone to conduct his business.'

'You mean he's still drunk?'

'Just that, Hamish.'

'Good grief, and the surgery left without a doctor. There's only the one most days.'

Hoynes tapped his nose with the stem of his pipe. 'That's where you'd be wrong.'

'How so?'

'For, knowing his brother would be in trouble with the health board and he'd likely lose his job, Ross – the lawyer, mind – put on the white coat and filled his place.'

It took Hamish a few moments to come to terms with this information. But when he did, a look of alarm crossed his face. 'You're saying that Ross is posing as the doctor?'

'Aye, you're quick, right enough. That's just what I'm saying.'

'My mother was at the surgery the day before last. You don't think she had a consultation wae the lawyer instead and never knew anything aboot it?'

'Aye, that's exactly the case, Hamish.' Hoynes took a contemplative puff on his pipe and eyed his crewmate grimly. 'I hope your mother's ailment wasn't of a *personal* nature?'

'What dae you mean?'

Hoynes raised an eyebrow and said no more.

'Oh, right. I get you, skipper.' Hamish's face reddened. 'Man, it was of a very personal nature, now you come to mention it.'

Hoynes shook his head. 'I'm sorry to hear it, Hamish. To be honest, I think it's a case of letting sleeping dogs lie. There's no need to worry the woman unnecessarily.' He took another puff. 'Though she'll be fair affronted when she finds oot. Goodness knows what your poor mother exposed to that imposter, all the time thinking he was a legitimate man o' medicine.'

'She'd to take off her stockings and put her leg up in a contraption, I know that much.' Hamish's face was pale.

'For any's sake. Say no more, Hamish, for I get the picture more than adequately. Just stop there, man.'

'Under the circumstances, she should have been saying that to McMurdo – whichever one it was.'

'You have the right o' it there, right enough.'

'She's had this problem for a good while now. It's that bad she walks wae a limp sometimes.'

'She does? The poor soul.' Hoynes looked surprised.

'Aye. She says the doctor gave her cream. You know, to soften it up before he tries to cut it oot.'

'Damn it, Hamish! I'm feeling quite bilious. You can spare me any further details.'

'She had me rubbing it wae a warm cloth the other night. You know, to ease the pain and that.'

Hoynes's concerned expression had now morphed into one of genuine shock. 'Now, son, I know you wear your heart on your sleeve, but what goes on in your ain hoose is a matter for you both. My advice is not to mention this to another soul, you hear me?'

'Och, it was fair throbbing, so in the end I sprayed it wae some disinfectant and wrapped a plaster roon it.'

Hoynes turned a whiter shade of pale. 'You know, Hamish, I confess I've taken a right notion for a dram after hearing your tale of woe.'

'It shows the quality o' man you are, Sandy.'

'How so?'

'Just the thought o' one woman's suffering wae an ingrown toenail is enough to stop you feeling sorry for yourself and get you back on the straight and narrow.'

'An ingrown toenail, you say?'

'Aye, it's fair been giving her gyp this last wee while.'

Breathing a sigh of relief, Hoynes struck a match and put the flame to the bowl of his pipe, which had extinguished itself during Hamish's torrid tale.

'Still, I'm no' happy about the McMurdo twins. They're professional men. Surely they should know better. Who told you about this caper, Sandy?'

'It was Nessie Watson that spotted something was awry. She was at school wae the pair o' them. Twins might be identical by definition, but when you see them every day throughout your time in education, well, you get to recognise certain individual traits, mannerisms and the like. She was fair adamant aboot the whole thing.'

At this point, Hamish was ready to comment that Nessie Watson had glasses as thick as milk bottles. In his opinion, at least, he felt it unlikely she'd be able to spot a trait or mannerism at a distance of two inches. Still, the whole subject seemed to have reinvigorated Hoynes, so he thought the better of any further comment.

'Anyway, it's good to see you, Hamish.'

'And you, Sandy. I've been down to Galbraith's slip every morning, just like you asked. Still no sign of that part.'

'It's just damnable, that's what it is. What's auld Galbraith got to say for himself?'

'The usual stuff about it being a bad time o' year, what wae the post being busy and all.'

'Typical of the man. He has the best collection of excuses under the sun.'

'He did mention that a fella had been admiring the *Girl Maggie*. Said he'd buy her in a trice. The bloke has plenty coin, by the sound o' things.'

'What bloke?'

'Galbraith didna say, and I didna ask.'

Hoynes sat bolt upright in his bed. 'I know fine who it will have been!' He stroked his ample beard. 'Right. Tomorrow morning at nine, meet me at Galbraith's slip.'

3

Thankfully, the next morning when Hamish opened his bedroom curtains, the rain had gone. In fact, the sun was out, and he could see a layer of frost sparkling on grass, walls and trees. He selected a warm knitted scarf to wear for his trip to Galbraith's slip.

In the kitchen, as was her morning habit, his mother was busy at the stove.

'Good morning, son. And what are you aboot today?'

'I'm meeting Sandy at the slip. He's no' happy about the time it's taking to fix the boat's engine.'

'And that's no' all he'll be unhappy about, I venture.'

'What dae you mean?'

'I hobbled down the street yesterday – wae my stick, you understand.'

'Aye.'

'I was in the greengrocer's when I saw a man that I'd forgotten existed.'

Hamish thought on this for a moment. He'd read in the *Fishing News* about elderly people losing their faculties. In the case of the article he'd perused, an old skipper had set out alone on his lobster boat and completely forgotten where his creels were or how to get back home. Being a worrier, Hamish was concerned that his mother's absentmindedness may be the first sign of something similar.

'Who was this body, mother?'

'I knew him in school. He was a couple of years ahead of me, but he fair turned heads wherever he went.'

'A looker, eh?'

'No such thing. He was a long streak o' misery back in those days. Mind you, when I saw him in the shop, he was smiling like the Cheshire cat.'

'Dreich MacCallum, I'll wager,' said Hamish instantly.

His mother frowned. 'How on earth would you know the man? He left the town when I was a lassie. As far as I know, this is his first time back in . . . och, it must be fifty years.'

'Sandy has himself in a state about him.'

It was his mother's turn to think. She stirred a pot of porridge absently until realisation dawned on her. 'There was an incident between that pair just before Dreich left Kinloch. I've been trying to remember what happened. I'd go so far as to say that Hoynes frightened the poor lad into exile.'

'Don't be daft. This is Sandy we're talking about.'

She ladled some porridge into a bowl, stirred in a teaspoonful of salt and placed it in front of Hamish on the table. 'You're too young to realise, but some folk change as they get older. Sandy Hoynes is a fine example.'

'I'm no' stupid enough to believe that he was born wae a pot belly and a big grey beard, if that's what you mean, Mother.'

'That's no' it at all, son. Sandy's no' the man you see today. Oh aye, he was every bit the rogue then as he is now. But your skipper was quite fiery as a lad.'

'Temper, you mean?'

'Just so, Hamish. Man, he'd a right quick temper. Accused

Dreich o' all sorts. The poor lad was fair affronted. It likely drove him away.'

'What kind of thing did he accuse him of – Sandy, I mean?'

She thought for a moment. 'Well, there was the boat race. It must have been after the Great War. We'd lost so many men, and those that were left were either old or too tired out wae fighting and the miseries o' conflict to be worried about a daft wee boat race. So they made it the preserve of youth. Young lads competed.'

'Aye, go on. What happened?'

'I canna mind the details at such a distance now. But it's fair to say that your skipper lost to Dreich MacCallum. He made such a fuss, accused Dreich o' cheating – the whole thing went on and on. To be honest, Sandy Hoynes couldna bear to be beaten fair and square. His mother and father were affronted at his carry-on. But there was worse to come.'

'There was?'

'Aye, there was. In those days, they handed out the seamanship certificates – I canna mind what they called them – to five young lads every year. They had to sit exams and the like.'

Hamish thought on this and considered himself lucky that such a restrictive practice was no longer in place. If it had been, the added element of competition, as well as the pressure of the exam hall, would have prevented his passing any nautical exams – ever. 'Go on, Mother. You're dreadful for heading off on a tangent when telling a tale. Aye, and you rarely reach your destination.'

'Listen tae you! I can just picture you in fifty years' time, sitting in that County Hotel spinning yarns for drams, just the way your auld grandfaither did.'

'I'll have grandweans to dandle on my knee, never mind yarns and drams.'

Hamish's mother cast him a baleful glance. She worried that he hadn't settled down. What lonely life was ahead of her only son, whiling away the hours all alone? She wouldn't last for ever. And the trials of life were best faced with a companion.

'I know what you're thinking,' said Hamish. 'I'll find the right girl, just you wait.'

'You'll no' find her in the County wae Hoynes, Peeny and the likes. You'll be an old man before your time.'

'Don't you worry about that. I have a plan.' Though he did his best to sound confident, Hamish felt anything but. There seemed to be a distinct lack of young ladies willing to walk out with him. This, plus his diminishing hairline, made him wonder that he may just not be the marrying type. 'Anyway, get on wae the tale, woman.'

She sighed. 'Well, as I remember it, Sandy failed miserably and concocted this great tale about the fishery officer conspiring to award the certificate to Dreich and no' himself. There was a right stink about it all. Hoynes was a laughing stock, and that's a fact.'

Hamish was loyal to his skipper. After all, had it not been for the offer of a berth on the *Girl Maggie* when his own father had been forced to sell his boat, Hamish wasn't sure there'd have been a place at the fishing with his name on it. Yes, Hoynes ribbed him about this and that, but he had a great affection for the man, considering him something of a surrogate father. The thought that his skipper had tried to cheat his way into a seamanship certificate, or whatever it was, left him strangely disappointed. And though he tried to mark the whole thing down to youthful indiscretion, he didn't manage to convince himself.

Whatever the truth, he had to meet Hoynes at Galbraith's slip in half an hour. After another helping of porridge and a second cup of tea, Hamish was ready to face the day. But, he mused, he wasn't entirely sure he was quite so prepared to face his skipper.

4

Hamish crossed the roundabout at the bottom of Main Street, passed the Weigh House, and made his way along the promenade to the slip. He was glad of the scarf he'd wrapped round his neck, for it was bitterly cold. Still, the loch was as deep a blue as the sky, in which gulls wheeled and called, and Hamish drew deeply at the smell of the sea. There was nothing like it for clearing the head. And mixed with the frosty air, he felt invigorated as he neared the *Girl Maggie*. He always thought of her as a fine vessel. But now, even he had to admit that, removed from her natural element, sitting on rails on the slip, she did look rather odd, even on the tubby side.

At first, he thought he was alone, until he heard voices coming from the other side of the fishing boat and spotted a tell-tale cloud of smoke appearing over the vessel's prow: Sandy Hoynes's pipe, to be sure.

As he rounded the prow, Hamish saw Galbraith and Hoynes in a heated discussion amidships. Galbraith was pointing up through the bottom of the boat, clearly indicating his displeasure.

'I don't know how you've kept her afloat all these years, Sandy,' said Galbraith, a man of average height with similar features.

'I beg your pardon,' Hoynes replied indignantly. 'This is one of the soundest vessels in the fleet, and no error.'

'You're deluded, man. All I can say is that I've kept your pumps in good order. They must be working harder than the engine, the bilge you're carrying.'

'It's merely ballast. She doesn't sit right in the water unless she's carrying some weight. A boat like this is fine-tuned to a high degree.' Hoynes took an extra-long draw of his pipe.

'What about this, then?' Galbraith reached above his head and poked his right index finger between two planks on the underside of the boat. 'Man, you can near get your fist in there, such is the gap. It's my assessment these planks are rotten.'

'I plug that wae oakum. There's no' a vessel afloat in which oakum doesna play a vital role.'

'True, Sandy, very true. But everybody else uses it for lining the decking, no' plugging great holes. Man, I'd love to see the ball o' the stuff this requires. It must be the size o' a melon!'

'Listen,' Hoynes pointed the stem of his pipe in Galbraith's direction, 'I'm paying you to fix the engine. If I wanted the advice of a shipwright, I'd ask one.'

'Fine.' Galbraith bent his knees and picked up a piece of rusted metal from the ground beside him. 'What would you say this was, Sandy?'

'You're the mechanic, you tell me.'

'Well, in all my thirty years o' being around engines in fishing boats, cars, lorries, motorbikes and the like, I've never seen anything like it.'

'Where did you find it?' Hoynes was pleased that this mystery was distracting the engineer from the poor state of the *Girl Maggie*'s superstructure.

'From the floor of your engine room, Sandy. It was in three inches o' water, so likely you missed it.'

'Is that the thing I've been tripping over the last couple o' years?' said Hamish.

Hoynes shot him a wicked glare.

'This'll be it, Hamish. I don't suppose you have any idea what it is?' said Galbraith, holding the metal up like a trophy.

'I'm no' just sure, I have to admit.'

'I think the mair worrying thing here is that you don't know what it is, Angus.' Hoynes shook his head. 'After all, there's no' a creature that comes oot o' the sea that I canna recognise. Is that no' right, Hamish?'

'There was that thing we hauled up in oor nets just off Plada, Sandy. You telt me you'd bugger-all clue what it was.'

'It was a rotting sheep, Hamish. Don't be daft.'

'It had two heids!'

'You're a terrible man for exaggeration.' Hoynes tamped more tobacco into the bowl of his pipe. 'It just looked as though it had two heids. In actual fact, it just had the one, rotted away a bit.'

'How come it had four eyes, then?' said Hamish, eager to defend himself.

'I've no' got the time to stand here talking aboot the flights o' fancy you pair have out at sea,' protested Galbraith. 'The mind boggles. I've got cars to fix back at the garage.'

As the argument continued, Hamish spotted a smart holiday cruiser tied up at the New Quay. Though she was around the same length as the *Girl Maggie*, her sweeping white lines made her look like something out of the space comics Hamish read. If this was the future of sailing, Hamish liked what he saw.

'I see you taking in that cabin cruiser, Hamish,' said Galbraith during a cessation of hostilities.

'She's a beauty, and no mistake.'

'All skim and bluster,' said Hoynes sourly. 'Underneath it'll be as fragile as a newborn. No' fit to face a decent wave, I'll venture.'

'Not true, Sandy. Not true at all. The owner let me aboard to see her engines yesterday. Engineered in Italy, would you believe? He says she can reach near thirty knots.'

'Man, if we stoated aboot at that speed, we'd frighten off every fish left in the sea. It's stealth we're after in our business.' Hoynes clamped the pipe between his teeth and put a match to the bowl. After a few puffs he saw fit to comment further. 'Mind you, I wouldn't say no to a leaf out o' the bank book o' the owner. Likely mair money than sense. One o' they pop stars that Hamish goes on aboot when he's in his free love moments, likely.'

'Not at all,' said Galbraith. 'In fact, she's owned by a local man – albeit he's been away from Kinloch for years. Nice chap – a ship's captain, no less.'

There followed the kind of pause Hamish had read about in books. Everyone stood stock-still: Galbraith awaiting a response, while Hoynes appeared to be chewing his pipe stem, jaws working furiously.

'You look as though you're about to blow a gasket, Sandy,' said Galbraith.

'The man you speak of – he's the one you were showing round my vessel the other day?'

'I was hardly showing him round. We were passing the time o' day. That's all.'

'I'm no' paying you to pass the time o' day, Angus. I'm

losing money hand over fist every day my boat is up here like some great exhibition. Maybe you should charge folk to come and have a gander, eh?'

Through the cool morning air, the tinkling of a bell could be heard. Wattie the postman was on his bike, heading towards them at speed, waving one arm. There was a parcel wedged into the basket on the handlebars.

'Mr Galbraith, here's the thing you've been waiting on,' said Wattie as he dismounted the bike. Helpfully, Hamish held it upright as the postman grabbed the parcel and handed it to the engineer.

Galbraith went about the package with a penknife he produced from the pocket of his boiler suit. It proved to be a metallic object about a foot in length with a spring at one end, tapering to a point at the other.

'Is that what's been holding us up? said Hoynes.

'The very thing.' Galbraith examined the engine part with a nod of satisfaction. 'I can have it fitted in a couple of hours, but you'll need to give me peace.'

'At your earliest convenience,' said Hoynes. 'Hamish and I can go and take the air while you're about it. When d'you think she'll be back in the water?'

Galbraith looked at the watch on his grubby, oil-stained wrist. 'Around lunchtime, I'd say. But remember, this isna an exact science.'

'Given the amount of time I've been waiting, I'm sure you'll do your best. We'll leave you to it,' said Hoynes.

Hamish watched Wattie the postman cycle off at speed. It was the kind of job he might have fancied, had he not managed to continue with his maritime career. Though he'd always worried about finding the correct addresses. It was a strange phenomenon, but at sea, he instinctively knew where he was going. On land, the whole process seemed more difficult. He comforted himself in the knowledge that Sandy Hoynes suffered in a similar manner. In fact, he recalled Mrs Hoynes saying that her husband could find his way from the house to the boat and back again, via the County Hotel, and that was about it. Hamish felt sure that this disparity between land and sea must be as the Good Lord intended. He and Hoynes took to the promenade and strode back into the town.

'I'm no' too sure about this "taking the air" business, Sandy,' said Hamish. 'It's on the cold side for traipsing about the streets.'

'I'm sure you've never learned a thing from me, Hamish. It's ten o'clock – we'll be sure to get an early dram in the County.'

'Man, you've fair bounced back after two weeks in your bed, skipper.'

'Maybe I was just needing some rest and recuperation. Have you ever thought o' that?'

'Nothing to do wae Dreich MacCallum, then?'

Hoynes took a couple of puffs of his pipe. 'I'd thank you not to mention that name again, Hamish. I'm sick o' hearing it. The sooner he returns to wherever he came from, the happier I'll be.'

The pair turned the corner and strolled on towards the County Hotel.

5

A small parade of guests were gathered at the County's reception desk, ready to check out. A large man with a pendulous belly was first in the queue, checking his watch with an impatient shake of his head.

'Good morning to you all,' said Hoynes, with what could best be described as a disarticulated bow.

The man waiting at the reception desk eyed him with contempt.

'My name is Waring – Geoffrey Waring. Are you the owner of this establishment?'

Hoynes looked about in faux confusion. 'Are you talking to me?'

'Well, I'm not talking to that gormless lad tagging along behind you, am I?' Mr Waring was an outspoken Yorkshireman, judging by his accent.

'I'll have you know that my first mate is one of the finest young fishermen on the West Coast, sir.'

'In that case, he cheats his appearance. Either that, or the rest of them leave a great deal to be desired. And I note that you haven't answered my question. Are you responsible for this . . . place?'

'I believe the word "gormless" refers to a person lacking

in sense or initiative. A foolish man, perhaps. Would you agree?'

'Though I'm surprised to say it, you're right.'

Hoynes tamped down some tobacco into his pipe. 'In that case, do you think I look like the owner of the hotel? I mean, a stout jumper, Breton cap and these yellow Wellington boots are hardly the garb of a man who runs such an establishment, wouldn't you say?'

'A smart arse. Just the thing I didn't want.'

'What did you expect?'

'An explanation as to why my bed sagged in the middle and my breakfast wasn't fit to feed a sparrow.'

'Och, you'll no' be needing the owner of the hotel to answer that.' Hoynes puffed yet another pipe into life.

'Why so?'

'Because any bugger can see that with the girth you're carrying, only a bed made of concrete would fail to sag in the middle. That aside, the paucity of your breakfast – if that was indeed the case – likely saved you from a coronary. Good day to you, Mr Gormless.'

A young woman in the queue giggled as Hoynes and Hamish made for the bar, while Waring spluttered and failed to find a suitable retort.

'You didna miss him, Sandy.'

'I canna stand such an attitude. And in any case, you're no' gormless, Hamish. Slow is a much more appropriate description.'

As Hoynes pushed the door to the bar open, Hamish smiled. The smile continued until he thought a bit longer about what Hoynes had just said. His expression turned into a frown.

In keeping with the time of day, the place was quiet. An elderly couple sat at a table at the back of the room, sharing a pot of tea. At the bar, almost as though they were fixtures, stood Peeny and Malcolm Connelly.

'Dear me,' said Connelly. 'It's the dry-land sailors.' The pair of them chuckled.

'Just ignore them, Hamish. Any man that thinks it fine to indulge in strong drink at this time of day isna worth listening to.'

'In that case, you'll be having tea, Sandy?' said Peeny.

'I'll have you know I've barely touched a drop o' the hard stuff in the last fortnight, Peeny.'

'Doctor's orders, I take it? The poor bugger will have to wring your liver oot wae a mangle.'

'Nothing o' the kind. And anyway, I've lost my faith in the local medical profession, given that you're more likely to encounter a lawyer than a doctor.'

This engendered a consensus amongst those gathered. Sandy and Hamish found a seat at a table as the elderly manager arrived behind the bar and took them in balefully.

'Man, the fleet's thirsty this morning, eh?'

'Fishing is a thirsty business. Hamish and I will have a dram each, when you've had your fill of ridiculous observations, thank you.'

And so, an interlude in the County began in much the same way that it always did. Peeny and Connelly wondered about Hoynes's absence and the wellbeing of the *Girl Maggie*, while the vexed subject of the McMurdo twins and their lack of professional ethics proved to be one upon which everyone could agree.

When they'd exhausted the many and varied ways a lawyer

performing the tasks of a clinician could lead to almost certain death, Peeny eyed Connelly with a wink.

'You were saying you've just been down the quay, Sandy?'

'That I have, and fair bracing it was. The weather's turning more seasonal, for sure.'

'You'll have seen that beautiful cabin cruiser at the pier, eh?' Peeny smiled guilelessly.

Hoynes took another sip of his dram. 'I'm sure I don't know what you mean. I was there to check on the progress o' my own vessel, no' worry aboot everyone else's.'

'Bonnie she is, right enough,' said Connelly. 'They say she can do near thirty knots. Can you imagine?'

'I'd like to see her hauling in a good catch, right enough,' said Hoynes. 'Man, she'd be low in the water wae a couple o' herrings and a lobster creel, I reckon.'

'You're no' purchasing a boat like that to go fishing, I don't think, Sandy,' said Hamish.

Hoynes kicked his second-in-command under the table. 'Man, I'm reconsidering my definition o' the word gormless, Hamish. Right now, I reckon it could mean a balding fisherman in his thirties, with grim career and life prospects into the bargain.'

'Let the lad speak, Sandy,' said Peeny. 'He has the right of it. I remember Dreich MacCallum just as well as you. And without taking into account the situation between him and your good self, I'd like to say a dourer boy never left this toon.'

'Aye, like a night oot wae the Grim Reaper,' said Malcolm Connelly in agreement. 'I wouldna fret on his massive success and riches, if I were you.'

Hoynes leaned back in his chair. 'Maybe it's time to let

sleeping dogs lie. I hadn't thought about the man for fifty years until he appeared in here a couple o' weeks ago.'

'Mrs H says you only speak about him when you're in a bad mood or drunk,' said Hamish.

Peeny and Connelly were doing their best to keep a straight face. They resorted to the old trick of holding their glasses to their mouths pretending to drink in order to cover their mirth.

'You pair would find a deid haddock amusing,' said Hoynes. 'I may be prepared to leave the past in the past, but I'll never forget what that imposter did. He set me back two years. I didna have the heart to sit the navigation exam the following year. After all, it had been stolen from me in a most wicked way.'

'No' to mention the race, eh?' said Connelly.

'It was a fine pointer to what a rascal we had in our midst. Goodness knows what he'd have been up to if he'd stayed in Kinloch. We were better rid of him, and no mistake,' said Peeny.

The door to the bar swung open once more. Framed in it was a tall, cadaverous man, with a shock of grey hair. His expensive brogues, well-cut sports jacket and tanned face were enough to identify him as comfortably-off. He stood before the gathered drinkers for a while, his expression a mask of abject misery.

'Dreich,' said Peeny. 'Man, I knew you were back in town, but it's still a surprise to see you.'

Dreich nodded solemnly, then did something few of them expected. A huge smile broke out on his face, and by the time he'd reached the bar he was beaming from ear to ear.

'A drink for my good friends,' he said in a heavily anglicised accent with only the merest trace of his hometown. He looked round the room. 'Sandy, I'm glad to see you're up and about again. We enjoyed a few drams the night I arrived, right enough. It's a shame you don't have the stomach for it. But I note it's doing its best to rise to the occasion.' He nodded to Hoynes's ample belly.

'Man, you've found your wit,' said Connelly, in truth rather amazed by the transformation in the man he'd known as a dour schoolboy.

'When you're the captain of a top-of-the-line cruise ship, a certain amount of bonhomie is expected.'

'Is that what you're at these days?'

'Forty years before the mast, Peeny. I missed this old place for a while, but I soon realised that leaving was the best thing I'd ever done. I worked my way up from deck boy. In seventeen years, I was a captain. And that's what I've done ever since. But I thought Sandy would have filled you in with all this, given he was here the night I arrived.'

Hoynes sipped his dram. 'Och, as you say, I've been a bit poorly the last couple of weeks. But I thought you'd have met up wae these rascals before now.'

'This isn't just a nostalgic trip, Sandy. I've been busy.'

'Busy at what?'

Dreich tapped his long nose. 'You'll see. But it might help bring this rundown old town into the twentieth century.'

'Are we going to get traffic lights?' said Connelly.

'Sorry?'

'You know, for the traffic in Main Street. Man, it's a nightmare trying to get out of Long Road.'

'The man's just telt you he's the captain o' a cruise liner. Why on earth would he be doon here to oversee the installation of traffic lights, Malcolm?' said Hoynes.

Connelly shrugged. 'Well, you never know.'

'No, I'm thinking that Captain MacCallum is here on matters o' a maritime nature. Would that be right, Dreich?'

'You are absolutely correct, Sandy. I can't say too much about it right now. But it will change this place for ever. You won't need to rely on the fishing. That'll soon be a thing of the past.'

There developed what could only be described as a chilly silence. The prospect of their beloved fishing being rendered obsolete by whatever Dreich MacCallum had up his sleeve was too much for the gathered mariners.

'There will always be fishing in Kinloch,' said Hamish eventually.

'No need for a young man like yourself to be worried, Seamus. You'll be much better off working for me. And anyway, fish stocks won't last for ever, not the way you're all plundering the sea.'

'The lad's name is Hamish,' said Sandy. 'And he works for me.'

'And how long will you carry on in the wheelhouse, Sandy? Peeny and Malcolm here have already hung up their nets. You should follow suit. A man in your condition won't last for ever.'

The collective intake of breath made the elderly couple drinking their pot of tea look up. Peeny stared at Connelly, Hamish glared at Dreich, and Connelly blew out his cheeks as he waited for a response from Hoynes.

'I'll have you know that I'm in fine physical condition. You canna face the ocean in all her many moods every day o' life without being ready for the challenge.'

Dreich smiled again, an unpleasant thing that didn't suit

his dolorous features one bit. 'It's a couple of pillows hidden up your jumper, then?'

'I'm heavy-boned, MacCallum. And unless you want a repeat o' what happened all these years ago, you'll shut your face.'

Hamish was surprised. He'd seen his skipper in many states of agitation, but never had he witnessed him threaten anyone with violence, if indeed that's what he'd just done. The atmosphere remained tense as Dreich stood at the bar and tossed back his dram with no comment. The whole scene reminded Hamish of a western he'd seen at the pictures a few weeks before – the gunslinger, a stranger, silent but menacing, finishing his drink before shooting up the bar.

Dreich put down his empty glass deliberately. He turned to address Hoynes. 'I'll tell you what, Sandy. Talking of old times, and if you're so hale and hearty, why don't we repeat our race?'

'You mean row to the island and back?'

'Yes. But let's make it more interesting. How about we race to Kilconnan rock and back. After all, we were just wee boys way back then. Now we're men, we can surely row a bit further.'

Hamish whispered to Hoynes under his breath. 'Sandy, that's a round trip of about five miles. You'll never manage to row a distance like that.' He was about to remind his skipper that the last time they'd been in charge of a rowing boat was when they'd been ashore at Lochranza. Hamish being rather in his cups, Hoynes had taken it upon himself to row back to the boat anchored out in the bay, just past the castle. By the time they got back to the *Girl Maggie*, Hoynes was so out of breath he had to wait for half an hour before he attempted to take the rope ladder up the side.

'Sorry, but you're not on, Dreich. I have to say, I'm surprised that a man like you – a ship's captain – would countenance such a ridiculous notion. We may have been wee boys back then, but now we're old men.'

'Oh, well, that's a pity. You may be happy to sink into old age . . . I'm not,' said Dreich.

'Madness, sheer madness. You've done the right thing, Sandy. A younger man would find it chore enough rowing that distance against wind and tide,' said Peeny.

'I'll be right busy over the festive period. My boat's about to go back in the water. I've no time for frolics of such a frivolous nature,' said Sandy.

'You've made your point, Hoynes. Just a pity we'll not have that rematch.' Dreich winked at Sandy.

'Aye, you're a wise man, right enough, Sandy,' said Connelly. 'It's fine enough today, if bitterly cold. But as yous all know, at this time o' year, the weather can turn on a sixpence.'

'There's such a thing as the shipping forecast. Or are you gentlemen still licking your finger and holding it in the air to predict the weather?'

'Ach, I've made my decision, and that's that,' said Hoynes. 'Let's get onto more important subjects.'

'Enough's enough, eh?' said Dreich. 'Oh, well, after that disappointment, who wants to come down to the pier and have a turn round the loch in my cabin cruiser? My wife Tabby is on her way from London today. I want to make sure it's shipshape for her. She likes her boats like she does her men: sleek, powerful and fast. Get my drift, Hamish?'

The young first mate blushed and said nothing.

'I've to go down and supervise Galbraith,' said Hoynes.

'Ah, your boat, Sandy. I had a look at her the other day.

I might make you an offer. She could be useful for my project.'

'No sale, MacCallum. She's a working vessel. But you're welcome aboard to see what good form she's in.'

That agreed, it was Hoynes's turn to buy another round. As he stood at the bar, Hamish studied Hoynes and MacCallum. Dreich was taller by a good four inches, but Hoynes was the wider. The *Girl Maggie*'s first mate was glad his skipper had made the right choice. Frankly, Hoynes was in no shape to be rowing anywhere.

6

The full round of drams had to be taken, each man buying the other a drink. So, it was a good while later that Hoynes, Dreich and the rest of the early morning drinkers made their way, somewhat haltingly, back to the harbour. This process was further delayed when Peeny slipped on black ice just outside Michael Kerr's bakery and had to be manhandled back to his feet.

As they turned onto the promenade, Hoynes was surprised to discover that not only was work on the *Girl Maggie* complete, but she was also being towed by an old tractor down Galbraith's slip ready to be moored against the pier.

'It's a fine sight to see, a proud vessel being restored to her natural element,' said Hoynes.

'It reminds me of the time I saw a dead whale being dragged off the beach in Newfoundland,' said Dreich.

Peeny looked at Connelly with an expression that indicated, *trouble ahead.*

By the time they'd walked to the slip, the *Girl Maggie* was afloat, Galbraith himself securing her to a stout bollard.

'Man, but that was quick, Angus,' said Hoynes.

'It took me near three hours. But I suppose time flies when you're having fun,' said the engineer. Judging by the all-pervasive aroma of whisky, this gaggle of mariners hadn't stinted on a dram or two.

Galbraith tugged at his oily cap and greeted Dreich. 'It's good to see you again, Mr MacCallum. Though I see you're not choosy when it comes to the company you keep.'

'Old pals, from way back in time,' Dreich replied.

'I think his memory is fair addled, Hamish. For none of us were his *pals* – the bugger never had any,' said Hoynes in a whisper. Then to Galbraith, 'If all is in order, I'm going to set her to the loch straight away by means of a sea trial.'

'As long as you pay me by the end of the week, you can take her to Australia for all I care.'

'You'll get your money. In the thirty years you and I have been doing business, have I ever let you down in matters o' a fiscal nature?'

The engineer rubbed his chin. 'No, I must say that you've paid every penny due.' And in a lower tone, 'Though "eventually" should be deployed in that sentence somewhere.'

Hoynes led the little party down the quayside and took to the ladder to access his fishing boat.

'It reminds me of that sea-clock at Greenwich,' said Dreich.

'What dae you mean?' said Hamish.

'It's a great ball that goes up and down a pole on the hour, and suchlike. I can't put my finger on it, but Sandy puts it in mind.' He grinned at Peeny.

Now on the deck of the *Girl Maggie,* Hoynes was back in his element. He beamed as he caressed the wooden frame of the wheelhouse. 'It's good to be back on board, old girl,' he said lovingly.

Though they'd all had a drink, one by one, the seafarers

took the ladder expertly. After all, for them, it was second nature.

Galbraith shouted down from the pier, 'Sandy, make sure and no' push her too hard. They didna send the right housing for that part that came wae the post. I had to fashion one on the fly, so to speak. She'll likely be fine, but take it easy at the start, just to be on the safe side.'

'He means don't go at your full pelt of three knots,' said Dreich with a laugh.

'He's fair changed, eh, Malcolm?' said Peeny. 'You couldna get as much as a giggle oot o' the bugger when we were young. Now it's like a Royal Command Performance.'

Connelly nodded his head. 'Some folk are like that. Look at my Margaret. She was a barrel o' laughs when I met her at first. Now, she's a right misery.'

'Aye, but staying wae you all these years is enough to silence anyone. Man, I get fair depressed just having a dram wae you.'

Connelly was about to reply when Dreich appeared at their side. 'Isn't she a beauty?' He pointed to his cabin cruiser tied to the pier opposite. 'Took her down to the South of France last year. It was like sailing with your slippers on. Just wait until you see inside, boys. You'll be fair wishing you abandoned the fishing and made something of yourselves like me.'

'No doubt,' said Peeny, not meaning it at all.

'I just wish I was you,' said Malcolm Connelly. 'The very thought of my many failings in life is sufficient to have me tying bricks to my ankles and jumping overboard. It would be a precious release.'

'You can scoff, Malcolm. But you'll eat your words when you're aboard. I even have a bar, you know.' Dreich marched off to torment Hoynes.

'You may well have a bar on your fancy cruiser, but you're still nothing but a scunner,' said Peeny. 'You'll no' have had the many rewards oor families and friends have bestowed on us.'

'Not sure that his family or friends have bestowed many rewards on him at all.'

Sandy Hoynes's head and shoulders were hanging out of the wheelhouse window. He was barking orders to Hamish, whose own head appeared now and again through the engine-room hatch further down the deck. 'Be sure and check the oil pressure, then we'll fire her up,' said Hoynes.

Dreich appeared below the window. 'It'll be a slow boat to China getting this old tub out of the harbour, Sandy.'

'There's many that think that, Dreich. But they're all wrong. It was only last year that I won a race oot into the loch wae a boat half her years in age.'

That unpleasant smile broke out across Dreich's face again. 'I remain to be convinced.'

'That's her ready, skipper. All in order in the engine room,' said Hamish, his oil-stained face emerging through the hatch.

'Leave that hatch open, Hamish. If I know Galbraith, there will be a surfeit o' lubrication oil to burn off. Better to let it vent.'

Hamish did as he was told then joined Dreich under the wheelhouse window.

'Is she shipshape, Seamus?'

'Aye, she's that and more.'

There was a chug, followed by a thud or two. Then something akin to a small explosion issued from the engine, sending a great cloud of black smoke through the hatch and the little chimney that abutted the wheelhouse.

'I knew it!' shouted Hoynes above the din. 'It's always the same when Galbraith has had his mitts on an engine.'

Though smoke still bellowed from the engine room through the open hatch, its colour became more grey than black. Shortly, the thudding and banging modulated into the gentler putt-putt of an engine in reasonable trim.

'Sweet as a nut,' said Hoynes, with no little pleasure. 'Untie her, Hamish, and we'll be off!'

The first mate dashed over the side, removed the rope from the bollard, and jumped back aboard the *Girl Maggie* with the grace of a ballerina.

'That's her ready for the off, skipper.'

Hoynes steered the vessel carefully away from the pier, pointed the prow roughly in the direction he intended to leave the harbour by, paused for a moment and pushed the throttle forward.

At first, nothing happened. But soon the gentle putt-putting increased in volume and frequency, as the *Girl Maggie* under Hoynes's command made for the gap between Kinloch's twin piers.

'Now we're talking, Dreich,' said Hoynes, his head poking back out of the wheelhouse.

'It's hardly Sterling Moss, is it?'

'Och, that's a different thing all together. You canna expect the same thing from a fishing boat that you can from a racing car.'

Dreich shrugged, though the shadow of a smile crossed his lips at Hoynes's efforts to impress him.

Galbraith looked on from the pier. He turned to Archie, the tractor driver. 'What on earth does he think he's doing? I telt him no' to push her until that new part settled in.'

'You know fine what he's like,' said Archie. 'The man's a bloody show-off.'

Despite this dismissive remark, Galbraith was chewing his lip as, in a flurry of smoke and thudding engine, the *Girl Maggie* approached the harbour mouth.

But just as Hoynes's attention was on the wheel, something odd happened. He felt the vessel shudder beneath him. There was a screaming noise, like the song of a steel hawser about to snap. The *Girl Maggie* appeared as though she had stopped in mid-stride. And though the engine was clearly in the process of slowing, the screeching noise continued. In fact, it grew to such a pitch that those aboard put fingers in ears to block it out.

Just as Hoynes was puzzling over what on earth was happening, there was a loud crack. A slim black object shot from the engine-room hatch like a bullet from a gun and soared into the clear blue sky.

'What's that?' said Peeny as he watched it gain height, causing seagulls to squawk and dive out of its way.

'It puts me in mind o' what might have happened in Cuba, had everyone no' seen sense,' said Malcolm, shading his eyes with one hand in order to follow its progress.

'What on earth happened, skipper?' said Hamish, visibly alarmed as he tumbled into the wheelhouse.

Hoynes had his field glasses trained on the unexpected projectile that had issued from his engine room. It was rapidly becoming a black speck in the blue, frosty sky.

'I'm no' right sure, Hamish. But there's something far wrong, that's certain.'

All aboard the *Girl Maggie* eyed its flight path. The object had almost disappeared, but, through his binoculars, Hoynes was first to notice its change of altitude. The projectile's progress slowed, it arced in the air as though caught by an invisible hand, and what had been an upward trajectory now reversed, as the forces of gravity came into play.

'What now, Sandy?'

'It's the old story, Hamish. What goes up must come doon!' Hoynes thrust his head from the wheelhouse. 'Take cover, everybody!'

As those present scattered about the fishing boat's deck, Hoynes, still peering through the binoculars, noticed that whatever had fired itself from his engine room had altered its angle of return. 'I think we're going to be fine. By the looks o' things it's going to land in the loch!'

Peeny was first to take note of this advice. The projectile was, once more, visible, and it appeared to be accompanied by a shrill whistling that was growing in intensity the nearer it came. 'It sounds like a Stuka!'

'Aye, but it's no' going to hit us, Peeny,' said Connelly. 'It's fair veered to the left. Hoynes may be right – it might come doon in the loch.'

'Aye, and it might no'.'

'Any chance o' the bloody thing hitting the fishery office?'

But just as the words left Connelly's mouth, the whistling noise became a scream and the impromptu missile appeared to accelerate through the thin winter air. Instinctively, everyone dropped to the deck. There was a large bang, followed by a crunching noise and the shattering of glass.

Hoynes got to his feet. His prediction had been wrong. Whether caught by the wind or simply propelled by the laws of physics, whatever had shot from the *Girl Maggie*'s engine room had landed on Dreich MacCallum's cabin cruiser with such force that it ploughed straight through, broke the vessel's back, and, in two perfect halves, sent it slowly sinking into the oily waters of Kinloch harbour.

7

Those aboard the *Girl Maggie* stood stock still. The shock of it all had rendered them mute and motionless.

It was only when Hoynes looked back at Galbraith's slip that he saw the engineer throw his cap to the ground and jump up and down on it.

'Mr Galbraith's no' looking too pleased, Sandy,' said Hamish meekly.

'This is his fault! If he'd done his job properly, we'd be oot in the loch without a care in the world.'

'Instead, you've sunk Mr MacCallum's cabin cruiser.'

As though he'd heard the comment, Dreich MacCallum recovered himself enough to shout up at Hoynes from the deck. 'You wait until I get my hands on you, Sandy Hoynes. That boat's worth a small fortune. At least ten times the cost of this heap!'

'Hamish, just slip the snib down on the wheelhouse door, will you, while I have a think. If Dreich breaks through, let him have it wae that claw hammer.'

The first mate looked on in horror. 'I think things are bad enough without me knocking MacCallum over the head wae a hammer, don't you?'

'Aye. But at least they might let us share the same cell in the gaol.'

As Hoynes predicted, Dreich MacCallum began hammering the wheelhouse door with his fist. 'Let me in there, Hoynes!' he roared.

'What are we to dae, skipper?' said Hamish through the din.

'I'm no' sure, but it'll likely involve Campbell the lawyer. Man, that could have killed someone, never mind wrecking that fancy cruiser o' Dreich's. We've faced many trials, Hamish, but this might prove to be the worst yet.'

Above Dreich's tirade, another sound could be heard. The voice was harsh and metallic, but Hoynes recognised it immediately.

'Sandy Hoynes, your vessel is blocking the entrance to the harbour. I'll have the *Evening Star* tow you to a berth. Then I want to see you in my office, do you hear?' Harbour master Mitchell's voice was plain as day through the megaphone.

✧

Mitchell, by way of the megaphone, persuaded MacCallum to cease his wailing. A tender had been sent to the side of the *Girl Maggie*, and now Hoynes was sitting across the desk from the harbour master, cap in hand.

'I don't need to tell you how serious this is, Sandy. You've destroyed an expensive vessel – that's bad enough. But you could easily have wiped out half the town. If the wind had caught that ... whatever it was ... we could have had folk felled all along the Main Street. And what would have happened if it had hit the fuel tanks?'

'Aye, but surely the crucial thing we should keep in mind

is that none o' these things *did* happen. Granted, Dreich's boat is at the bottom o' the sea. But he'll be insured. And to be honest wae you, I can hardly be blamed for this incident,' said Hoynes. He knew that he was stretching mitigation to breaking point. But he had to try.

'I've had to inform the Ministry. Aye, and the fishery officer.'

'Och, this had nothing in the least to dae wae fish, unless we have a shoal o' the flying variety in the loch. I'll speak to MacCallum, and we'll come to an understanding.'

'An understanding? Sandy, do you have any idea how much these cabin cruisers cost – thousands. You'll lose everything – and that's being optimistic. If the police get involved . . . man, they could be carrying you off in handcuffs.'

'Aye, and it nearly Christmas. So much for the spirit o' joy and forgiveness.' Hoynes pulled his pipe from the depths of his pea jacket and tamped some tobacco into the bowl, a slight tremble in his hands. 'What aboot Galbraith, eh? Man, that was a shoddy job, and no mistake. I expected him to fix the engine, no' install a ballistic missile.'

'But, Sandy, you pelted away from the pier as though auld Nick was after you.' Mitchell sighed. 'And you know full well what folk are going to say, don't you?'

'Plenty, if I know this toon.'

'They'll say you did this on purpose. Everybody and their friend knows that you and Dreich MacCallum have a *past.*'

'And they'd be right! The bugger diddled me oot o' my navigation certificate and cheated in a race. It's him you should be talking to. Man, he might be sailing the world without so much as a qualification.'

'I'm sure he's faced harder tests than the one you both sat as boys.'

'But you don't know that for a fact.'

'I'll have to write a report and take some statements. You'll have all and sundry wanting to speak to you, Sandy.'

'Aye, I dare say they will.'

'My advice is to find out where you stand legally. Go and see a lawyer.'

'I'd have been with auld Campbell this minute if we weren't sitting here chewing the cud like a couple o' fishwives.'

'Sandy, you sank a boat in the harbour for which I'm responsible. You surely can't think I'm going to let this go on a nod and a wink?'

'Well, I canna say I'd be averse to the idea, right enough.'

'It was only months ago that you threw an exciseman in the loch.'

'You canna blame me for that. He fair jumped in over the side of his own accord.'

'So you said at the time.'

Hoynes filled the room with pipe smoke. 'You can do me a favour, if you will.'

'Oh, what now?' Mitchell the harbour master was a former lobster fisherman, and although he could be stern, he was always on the side of his fellow mariners.

'Can you see where Dreich is, please?'

Mitchell stepped to the window of his office. Sure enough, MacCallum and Galbraith were staring forlornly over the side of the pier at what remained of the former's vessel.

'He and Galbraith are peering into the loch where his boat should be,' said Mitchell. 'I don't know what they're planning, but if it's salvage, they can forget it.'

'Good. Well, if you wouldn't mind giving me a quick hurl up to the lawyer in that fine motor car of yours, I'd be much obliged. I'm no shrinking violet, you understand, but at this stage, I think it prudent to avoid any altercation wae Dreich.'

'His wife's on her way from London, too – to see the boat. It's only just been refitted.'

'Just make matters worse, why don't you? Come on, let's get going.'

8

There was something about Campbell's office that Hoynes didn't like. It reeked of oppression and last chances, of dwindling hope in the heart of miscreants everywhere. Not that he was, by any means, a miscreant. What had happened was an accident, plain and simple. No man could have avoided it – or so he told himself.

The place was scattered with papers. They sprouted from drawers and filing cabinets, and lay in heaps across the old oak desk, behind which sat the elderly lawyer. He had rheumy blue eyes, a crumpled face and, clamped between his teeth, a cigar from which a length of ash drooped. Though Hoynes knew the man – had done all his life – he still brought to mind a Cockney spiv rather than a man of letters and the law. He was in his late seventies and looked every year of it.

'Sit down, Mr Hoynes.' Campbell took an ample draw of his cigar. 'I don't know what I'd do without these bloody things. They get me through the day – and a wee dram, of course.'

'Mr Campbell, I'll tell you true. Add a good fillet o' fish two or three times a week and you have the recipe for eternal life. I'm sure o' it.'

'You may be right, Sandy. It seems like yesterday I was

sitting at this desk opposite your late father. He was a fine man. I fancy you sail rather closer to the wind than he did.'

'As close as the wind will allow, sir. A man has to be on his toes to make a few bob in these straitened times, and no mistake.'

'Absolutely. My race is almost done, I'm glad to say.'

'Och, don't say that, Mr Campbell. I'm sure you have a year or two left in you, right enough.'

'I was meaning that my professional race is almost done, not that I'm about to breathe my last. I'm just waiting for my son to take over. He should be in place by March next year. So, you might be my last chance for fame. The young ladies in the office tell me you nearly killed half of Kinloch with a missile.'

'As I might have expected, exaggeration oot o' all proportion. It was a mechanical failure, nothing more, Mr Campbell.'

The old lawyer sat back in his chair. 'I'm all ears, Mr Hoynes, all ears.'

The skipper went on to describe that morning's events. Campbell grunted here and there, in order to feign interest. But as Hoynes came to the part of the story where the mechanical component shot from the engine-room hatch and took to the skies, his eyes widened, and he removed the cigar from his mouth. By the time the *Girl Maggie*'s skipper finished his tale with the sinking of Dreich MacCallum's pleasure cruiser, he threw back his head and laughed heartily at it all.

'My, Sandy, but you're a tonic on a cold day. I'd forgotten the lad had that nickname. They called his father the same thing. A more twisted, untrustworthy man never lived. I daresay his son is no better.'

'Not one bit, Mr Campbell, I assure you.'

Campbell stubbed out his cigar and rested his head on one hand. 'Tell me, Mr Hoynes, is your insurance up to date – for the boat and operation thereof, I mean?'

'I think so. I've never quite had cause to have much to do with the insurance company. Other than make sure the premiums are paid up on time, of course,' said Hoynes hurriedly.

'And as you describe it, the whole episode appears to be an unfortunate accident. Though you may have to implicate Mr Galbraith, if you believe his work to be sub-standard. I know that will be hard, considering how close the fishing community is in Kinloch.'

'Think nothing o' it, Mr Campbell. As far as I'm concerned, he's mair to blame than me. In my books, a man should dae his work with diligence and pride. It's clear to me Galbraith just bolts one thing to the next wae very little thought whatsoever.'

'I see. Good to know that misplaced loyalty won't be a problem here.'

Hoynes adopted an angelic expression. 'I could be preventing a calamity of a much more serious nature.' He placed his right hand on his chest. 'I feel it is my duty to the public rather than friends and business acquaintances, Mr Campbell.'

'Just so, Hoynes, just so.' He rummaged around the papers on his desk, managing to extract a large leather-bound diary from under the mess. 'I'm making a note here to check on some of the more arcane elements of maritime law and how it applies to this case. I hope you have no issue with me seeking testament from your guests aboard the *Girl Maggie* and other pertinent witnesses?'

Hoynes folded his arms. 'None at all.' He scratched his beard. 'Mind you, I'd steer clear of Dreich MacCallum.'

'Obviously.'

'And Peeny canna help but spin a tall tale or two. He'd likely embellish normal events into something extraordinary. The man should write books.'

'I see.'

'And Malcolm Connelly has a miserable home life. Fair scunnered he is, and that's a fact. Man, I think he'd come oot wae any sort o' nonsense for the sake o' amusement.'

'That doesn't leave many reliable witnesses on board, Sandy.'

'Well, there's Hamish.'

'I knew his father, too. I hope he doesn't suffer from a similar affliction?'

'Now you come to mention it, Mr Campbell, he can take a fair bucket. He has a noble thirst, would be a fairer way to put it. Och, and you know fine what young folk are like these days. He'll likely be up in the air on some concoction o' drugs or another.'

'I believe the term is "high".'

'There, you have the right o' it straight away, Mr Campbell. I'm forgetting you have a young son yourself. He'll likely be fair stoating aboot on the drugs. You'll have had plenty o' experience.'

'He's forty-seven, Mr Hoynes. Rather long in the tooth for such indulgences, wouldn't you say?'

'Man, how time flies. I remember him when he was just a wee lad doon the pier wae a fishing rod. Mind, it wisna me that booted him up the arse when his line got caught in the nets.' Hoynes directed his gaze to the floor, lest his eyes give him away in this particular instance.

'Good. It sounds to me as though, judging by the unreliability of the rest of the witnesses to this incident, it's mainly your word against MacCallum's. The cause of the mechanical failure must lie with Galbraith.'

'Very much so, Mr Campbell.'

'Who would have thought little Kinloch was home to such a parcel of rogues, eh?'

Hoynes nodded in agreement. But he saw fit to raise one index finger as a troubling thought crossed his mind. 'This information – all about the witnesses, I mean. It's between you and me – confidential?'

'Of course.'

'Aye, just so, as expected.'

'Unless, in the unfortunate event of an action, they are called by the other side, and I have to make your opinions of these people known to the court.'

'A court action?'

'Hopefully, it won't come to that, Sandy. But this MacCallum sounds as though he has a bob or two. You can never be too sure with the wealthy. But if everything is as you say it is, I feel we can reach an amicable conclusion to this problem. However, there may be considerable animus, as far as our friend the captain is concerned. I'd lie low until I sort things out, Sandy.'

'You're the man for the job, right enough. I'll no' keep you back. I daresay you'll need to spend the rest o' the day getting this office shipshape. That's bound to take up a few hours o' your time. It looks like thon part fae my engine landed here.' Hoynes stood, shook the lawyer's hand enthusiastically, then took his leave.

Campbell lit a cigar as he watched the fisherman close the door behind him. 'And you're the biggest rogue of them all, Sandy Hoynes.'

9

Sandy Hoynes shivered in the December chill as he made his way down Main Street. The big tree at the bottom of the road was being adorned with lights, and with the smoke from coal fires in the cold frosty air, the place was beginning to feel festive. But what kind of Christmas and New Year would be in store for him? At best, the inadvertent sinking of Dreich's boat would cost him money, at worst there could be a higher legal price to pay.

He had the notion for a dram but knew it would be foolish. It was then that Hoynes remembered his wife had asked him to pick up a couple of things from the shops. He thrust a hand into a pocket of his dungarees and produced the shopping note she'd entrusted him with earlier that morning.

It turned out that all she needed was a loaf of bread, some turnips and a tin of shortbread. It would make for an unusual supper, he thought. But he'd never had cause to question his wife's culinary skills.

As Hoynes made his way down the street, he saw Nancy and Agnes McGowan hobbling towards him. The sisters, of a certain age, were both on sticks. They were kind, well-thought-of women in the town. Long widowed, the fisherman made sure they didn't go without a fillet of fish or two every now and again.

'Good day to you, ladies. Are you out for a bit o' shopping before Christmas?'

Nancy – the elder of the two – glared at him. 'Aye, that was the plan. But since you launched an attack doon at the pier, we're heading home in case we get caught in the crossfire.' Her sister nodded in grim-faced agreement.

'Now, come on, Nancy. You know fine what like the gossip is in this place. It was a mechanical failure, nothing more.'

'Your backside, Sandy Hoynes,' said Agnes. 'Everybody and their friends knows you bear a grudge against Dreich MacCallum. Aye, and you're like an elephant, too. Decades you've been waiting to get back at that man, and you've succeeded. Some memory!'

'And by wicked means into the bargain,' Nancy added.

'None o' this is true at all, ladies.' Though he tried, Hoynes wasn't going to get a chance to speak.

'Norman MacLay telt us that you learned your skills in the Boys' Brigade,' said Agnes.

'What skills?'

'The making of bombs and the like. Well, I'm here to tell you, you'll no' be dropping anything on oor hoose.'

'This is ridiculous. Why don't you both come with me, and we'll get a nice cup o' tea down at the Copper Kettle? I'll even indulge you in a cake or two, eh?' Hoynes smiled at the pair.

'You can stick your cake where your mother never kissed you, Sandy Hoynes,' said Nancy. 'And you needn't bother offloading your auld fish on us. The cat will miss it, but I won't. In any case, I don't want wee Magnus being fed by a scunner like you.'

'You give the best fresh fish to your cat?'

'Watch out, Agnes. He's no' happy. Best we stay in the old bomb shelter tonight in case he drops one o' his missiles on us. Do you know what folk are calling you, Sandy?'

'No, but I could have a guess.'

'Doodlebug, that's what. And, come to think o' it, you've got the build, right enough.'

'Just so, Agnes. There's no' a body in the toon feeling safe this day, and that's a fact,' said Nancy. 'And we're just two o' them.'

With that, arm in arm, they shuffled off, leaving Hoynes in the street feeling most perplexed.

The situation wasn't much better in Michael Kerr's bakery. The young woman who served him was perfectly polite but eyed Hoynes with great suspicion. To the rear of the queue, customers were talking behind their hands.

As he left the shop, Hoynes heard a man's voice say, 'Aye, cheerio, Doodlebug.' It was clear that his worst fears had been realised. The unfortunate accident that had happened earlier that day was now growing arms and legs. Sandy Hoynes was rapidly becoming a pariah in his own community.

It was with great relief that he opened the door to Gilmour's the greengrocer and was greeted with a broad grin by the proprietor.

'How are you the day, Sandy?' said Duncan Gilmour, his hand cupped to his right ear in order to hear the reply.

'I've had better days, to be honest,' said Hoynes in a loud voice. The greengrocer was notoriously hard of hearing, so everyone had to speak up.

'You'll have heard about the basking shark that sunk a boat earlier this morning, eh?'

'No.'

'It was Davie MacClement that told me. I wisna quite catching the detail o' it, but apparently the bloody thing went sailing into a posh boat at the Old Quay.'

Hoynes pleaded ignorance. At the same time, he was well aware that the shopkeeper had just misheard his tale of woe.

Gilmour thrust two large turnips into a paper bag, which he spun round in both hands to twist closed. 'They're saying there's a search on for this fish. Davie reckons they'll gut it. I'm no' for harming such beautiful creatures, but it canna go aboot sinking boats. It's better put oot o' its misery.'

By the time his shopping transactions were complete, Hoynes felt utterly miserable. No doubt, people wanted to gut him. He had to get home; he needed time to think. He'd planned to catch the local bus, but judging by his reception at the shops, the best idea was to take the quiet route up to the scheme.

Sandy Hoynes, master mariner, fishing legend and erstwhile boat sinker, cut a dejected figure as he made his way up to the road with his little bag of groceries. The joy of the festive season might be settling on all and sundry, but for him the prospects were bleak.

10

Dreich MacCallum was sitting on his own in the little reception office of the County Hotel. He'd been trying to contact his lawyer in London since the demise of his cabin cruiser. But the man was proving elusive, and rather than feed coins into the public phone box, he'd asked the hotel management if he could use their facilities, for which he'd pay. They reluctantly agreed, and here he was, waiting for the hour to turn, and to call as he'd been instructed.

With a few minutes to spare, Dreich reflected on his decision to leave Kinloch, all those many years ago. Hoynes and his father had made much of the fact that he'd cheated them out of the navigation certificate, and his father had felt it would be best for his son to spend some time elsewhere.

He remembered the day he'd landed on the docks at Glasgow. There was the promise of a job from a distant cousin, but little more. He'd felt homesick and alone. But things had gone his way. He'd been employed as a junior hand on a small merchant vessel plying her trade from Scotland to Norway. At first, the tug of Kinloch was strong. But as he met new people and saw new places, his dislocation eased, and he soon revelled in being away from the gossip and scrutiny of his hometown.

As Dreich MacCallum looked around the lobby of the County Hotel, he realised almost nothing had changed since his first visit to the place as a boy. In fact, the whole town looked almost identical to the way he remembered it. He shivered at the thought of being stuck here, in the middle of nowhere, for a lifetime. And unlike many folk from Kinloch who found themselves living in other places, he didn't consider this place as home. No, that had been a long time ago.

He checked his watch and dialled the number on the card his lawyer had given him. The phone rang and was answered by a bright female voice.

'Chetlam, Morris and Fincher, can I help you?'

'Yes, Mr Fincher, please. It's Captain James MacCallum, I've been trying to contact him for most of the day.'

'Apologies, Captain MacCallum. He's been in court. I'll put you through straight away.'

Following a click, buzz and a short period of silence, Nigel Fincher's voice boomed from the telephone.

'MacCallum! How are you, old boy? Hope you're spending Christmas on dry land this year?'

'As it turns out, that's very much the case, Nigel.'

There followed Dreich's long description of what had happened that day. Though his depiction of events was reasonably accurate, it was heavily weighted against Hoynes, whom he painted as the villain of the piece.

Once the tale was complete, Fincher hesitated for a moment. 'I must say, this Hoynes chap sounds like the very devil. You've had a lucky escape, if you ask me. My advice would be to steer as far away from him as possible, if you intend to stay in this Kinlock for much longer.'

'It's Kin-*loch*,' said Dreich, still loyal enough to his old home to make sure its name was pronounced properly.

'Damn it, man, you can't expect me to attempt that. I'd choke. I'm of the opinion that one has to be born in Scotland to get your tongue round these guttural words. The bloody Welsh are just as bad. I was drenched by a male voice choir there once. As I recall, it was in a bar in Llanfairfechan . . .'

'Nigel, what are my options?'

'Well, entirely up to you, old boy. His insurance should cover the material loss. But if this chap's the rogue you describe, then perhaps you're as well to try some more punitive civil action – you know, for emotional distress, trauma and the like. I'll have to read up on Scotch law, of course. But there must be some recourse to compensation – above and beyond the initial material payment, you understand.'

'Cash, you mean?'

'Yes, cash, of course. But failing that, well, goods, property and suchlike.'

Dreich thought for a moment. 'Would a fishing boat count in this?'

'It'll depend on the court, but I see no reason why you shouldn't seek some recompense for inconvenience to you, not to mention the shock of it all. It sounds bloody terrifying. The law is very sympathetic to frightened people – on both sides of the border.'

'Right, in that case, I'll go for his fishing boat, the *Girl Maggie*. I'll sail that bloody tub out of Kinloch harbour for the last time.'

'Worth something, is she?'

'I doubt it. Fit for scrap. But it'll ruin Hoynes, and that's what I want to do more than anything.'

'Ha! I wouldn't like to come across you in a dark alley, MacCallum. I'll be in touch. It's this County Hotel, isn't it?'

'It is indeed, Nigel.'

With that, the call ended. Dreich placed the phone on its cradle and sat back, hands behind his head. It was all he could do to keep a wide smile of satisfaction off his face. He knew he'd run into his old enemy on his visit to Kinloch. Dreich hadn't thought much about him for years, but as soon as he spied Hoynes in the bar at the County Hotel, the old feelings returned. He remembered hating him when he was young. The lad was fair-haired and good looking. He caught the eye of the lassies with his easy wit and charm.

But Dreich MacCallum had won the day all those years ago, and he'd win it again.

'Are you finished wae the phone, Mr MacCallum?' said Maureen, the young receptionist. 'It's just I need to use it.'

'Yes, I'm all done here. Thank you very much for the facility. Be sure to add it to my bill. I better get ready for my wife's arrival. She comes off the bus at six.'

Dreich MacCallum swept out of the office, a spring in his step, and disappeared up the wide staircase to his room.

Maureen sat back behind her desk. She thought for a moment or two before consulting the local phonebook. She dialled a number and waited for a reply.

'Hello, two-seven-nine, can I help you?' The woman's voice was warm and friendly, with just a touch of concern.

'It's Maureen at the County Hotel, Mrs Hoynes. Is Mr Hoynes about at all?'

11

To say that the atmosphere in the Hoynes household was tense was putting it mildly. The man of the house was chewing on his pipe, a large dram by his side. Meanwhile, his wife was grating cheese, staring into the middle distance. So distracted was she, the cheese was flowing over the rim of the bowl positioned to contain it.

'There's cheese all o'er the floor, woman,' said Hoynes before taking a fair swallow of his dram.

'Aye, and I'll be lying in amongst it, the way I feel right now, Sandy. What on earth are we going to do?'

'Och, I don't know. The whole thing's grown legs, arms – aye, and a big heid. It was an accident, plain and simple. Aye, no' to mention Galbraith's shoddy workmanship.'

'Still, it was good o' wee Maureen to let us know. Lucky she heard Dreich on the phone.'

'I'm no' sure that *lucky* is the word I'd use aboot any o' this. *Desperate* is a more apt description, I'd say.'

A knock sounded at the door, and Marjorie Hoynes hurried off to answer it, casting a worried look at her husband as she did.

'It'll be Hamish, no' the Grim Reaper. Calm yourself, dear.'

Despite his bravado, Hoynes listened carefully to hear just who was at the door. But his prediction had been correct. Hamish burst into the lounge looking pale-faced.

'Is it true, Sandy – he wants the *Girl Maggie*?'

'So it would seem, son. Here, sit yourself down, and don't be standing there like a prophecy o' doom.'

'What are we to dae, Sandy?' said Hamish, now sitting on the edge of the settee.

'I have a plan, don't worry.'

'Oh, for heaven's sake,' said Marjorie. 'I'm going to phone the doctor and get some o' they Valium folk are going on aboot. I'm a nervous wreck. If it's no' bad enough he's sinking boats, now he's got a plan.'

Hoynes shook his head. 'You needna worry. I've got auld Campbell on the case right this minute.'

'But will Dreich no' have the best lawyer money can buy? No disrespect to Mr Campbell, but he's hardly in the first flush o' youth, Sandy.'

'That he certainly isna. But wae all those accumulated years comes experience. Dreich can have as fancy a lawyer as he likes, but he'll no' have been there and done it like Campbell.'

'That's your plan, then. Put your faith in a man that's near a hundred years old,' said Marjorie. 'I canna say I'm confident.'

'It's a terrible world,' said Sandy. 'Folk think as soon as you're over sixty your race is run. Well, I'm here to tell you, that's a lot o' rubbish.' He straightened his collar. 'Look at me, for instance. Still the finest fisherman on the West Coast, and I saw sixty a good while ago.'

'They say Ronnie Hervey up in Oban has been bringing in huge catches over the last couple o' years,' Sandy,' said Hamish.

'Och, fish are more plentiful up there. Everybody and his friend knows that. It doesna make him the best fisherman.'

'And that Wilson fella on Mull goes right oot into the Atlantic. I hear he's the most formidable navigator aboot.'

'What's he after, whales? There's no point heading away oot into the ocean. Man, you can catch all manner o' strange fish. My father was on a boat once that went away oot. Near at the Azores, they were.'

Marjorie rolled her eyes.

Undaunted, Hoynes continued. 'They hauled in this great fish. As big as a basking shark, she was.'

Unlike Mrs Hoynes, Hamish was all ears. 'What kind o' fish was that, Sandy? A tunny, maybe?'

'No, nor tunny. Nobody could identify the thing. They were all standing gawping at it when the thing raised its heid. "Put me back in the sea, this minute," it said. Aye, wae some authority, too. My faither told me he near had apoplexy. There was the fish, speaking the King's English, as plain as day. If I mind right, it had a bit o' a Spanish twang. But that's to be expected when you're as close to the Azores, right enough.'

'Stuff and nonsense,' said Marjorie.

'It's true, I tell you. They were so feart, the crew did exactly as they were told and threw the damn thing back o'er the side. Did it no' thank them when it was back in its natural element.'

'You'll be telling us it waved them goodbye next,' said Marjorie.

'Don't be ridiculous, dear. Any man knows that a fish canna wave. It's just no' physically possible. But my faither fancied that it swung its tail a couple o' times by way of a "cheerio" before it disappeared.'

Hamish mulled this over for a few moments before

continuing. 'I'm hearing there's a Macleod over on Islay that's a fine fisherman. Never lost for an abundant shoal, they say.'

'Well, that's nonsense right fae the start. Everyone knows fine that there's never been a good fisherman come off that island. Och, they're too immersed in whisky o'er there to steer, never mind catch a fish.' Hoynes took another gulp of his dram. 'In any case, Hamish, you're supposed to be here for moral support. So far, you've done nothing but tell me that near every fisherman on the planet is better at the craft than me.'

'I was just passing on what folk are saying.'

'In that case, haud your wheesht while I tell you my plan.'

'Here we go,' said Marjorie. Knowing her husband as she did, she was sure that what she was about to hear would be inventive. Successful? That was another matter.

'Hamish, you know auld Willie MacEachran.'

'The lobster man that broke his leg?'

Hoynes smiled. 'Aye, you have it straight away.'

'What about him?'

'He asked me the other day if I widna mind attending to his vessel. As you know, a good boat needs much care and attention, and he's no' capable at the moment, being on crutches.'

'I canna see how looking after someone else's boat will save the day, Sandy,' said Marjorie.

'That's no' the plan at all.' Hoynes turned to his first mate. 'Hamish, I want you to be at Dalintober pier at five tomorrow morning. We'll pick up the *Golden Dawn* then.'

'*Golden Dawn* is right, Sandy. Why on earth are we going to fix up the boat that early? Man, it'll be freezing.'

'Aye, and dark, too.' Hoynes winked.

Marjorie thought for a moment. 'I know what you're going to do. And if you think you can hide out in that lobster boat, you're wrong.'

'Och, that's just sheer nonsense. Folk would know the boat was missing. The whole fleet would be out looking for me.'

'What then?' said Hamish.

'I'm taking a wee holiday. Marjorie, where's that bell tent we used to go up the hill wae?'

'That auld thing? It's in the loft, where it's been for about twenty years.'

'Good. Hamish, you can help me get it down. I'm going to go camping for a while.'

'But it's nearly Christmas, Sandy.' Marjorie adopted an incredulous look.

'I'll be back by then, don't worry.'

'It's next week!'

'Listen, I just need time for Campbell the lawyer to come up wae something. Right now, I'm a sitting duck. Forbye, you canna charge folk wae any misdemeanour when they're away working hard and can't be contacted.'

'Busy doing what?' said Hamish.

'Taking Willie's boat out on sea trials.' Hoynes drained his glass. 'I've had enough o' folk looking at me as though I'm about to eat their weans. Aye, and I have to say, I'm a bit put out that folk have mair time for Dreich MacCallum than they do for me. And him a right scunner, too.'

'It just shows you, eh?' said Hamish. 'From hero to villain in a few hours.'

'I know fine, son.'

'And what will you eat? How will you stay warm, Sandy? It's December!' Marjorie bit her lip.

'And how do you think our ancestors survived the cold night, eh? They couldna just put a few more coals on the fire.' Hoynes pondered on this for a moment. 'Well, they likely could, but I'm no' right sure they'd invented coal back then.'

'Coal's been in the ground for millions o' years, Sandy,' said Hamish.

'Aye, I daresay it has. But it's no' been in one o' MacNeally's sacks for that length o' time. Tell me, if I asked you to go and find fuel supplies, what would you do? And don't say you'd be off to the coal merchant.'

'There's the pit at Machrie.'

'Now you're just being obtuse for the sake o' it, Hamish. The answer is simple.'

'What?' said Marjorie.

'Wood. There's piles o' the stuff all around. And where I'm going there's no shortage o' the stuff at all.'

'And where are you going?' said Hamish.

'Needs to be a place I can hide if some bugger happens along. A place wae wood, aye, and plenty o' it.'

'On the coast, Sandy?'

'Aye, on the coast, Hamish. Portroy beach is where I'll hide for a while. Dreich won't take my boat off me, and that's a fact.'

Marjorie wrung her hands. 'But why Portroy?'

'Easy. There's a good forest o' trees just up from the beach. Firdale isna far away in case of emergencies, and there's plenty places to pitch my tent behind big rocks and the like. And face it, who's going to be aboot Portroy beach at this time o' year, eh?'

'Only a fool,' said Marjorie.

'You're no' to be countenanced when it comes to plans,

Marjorie. Just pure misery, every time. Hamish can keep me supplied until it's safe to come back. As far as anyone is concerned, I'm off to Glasgow on business.'

'Is that before or after the sea trials, Sandy?' said Hamish.

'You're just complicating matters wae your attempts at hilarity. I don't care what Dreich tries to do, nobody is taking the *Girl Maggie* off me, and that's a simple fact.'

Marjorie looked at the determined cast of her husband's features. She could have argued that camping out with an ancient tent in the depths of winter was a ridiculous idea. But she knew her husband. Once he'd made his mind up, that was it – for better or for worse.

12

When his alarm burst into life at a quarter past four the next morning, the last thing Hamish had in mind was getting out of bed. When he sat up and put his bedside light on, he could see a great cloud issue forth as his breath froze before him on this bitterly cold day.

But he had his instructions. And since Hoynes was determined to take the course of action upon which he'd settled, as a loyal first mate it was his duty to be of any assistance he could.

Still, as he sat in front of two buzzing bars of the electric fire in the parlour, a cup of tea clasped between both hands, he wished he'd never heard the name Dreich MacCallum. But then he remembered how his father had lost his fishing boat, and how it had cut the man to the core. So much so that the drink, for which he had always been partial, took his life as he wallowed in the misery of it all.

Though Hamish tried to picture Hoynes in this predicament, he found it hard to imagine his skipper succumbing in such a way. Hoynes – even when things were at their darkest – managed to find solace in something, usually his wit and resourcefulness. Yes, there were many great fishermen in the fleet at Kinloch, but none matched Sandy Hoynes for his guile and willingness to think his way out of any dilemma.

But were Dreich MacCallum and his sunken boat a problem too far?

Putting on a vest, two jerseys, his pea jacket, a woolly scarf and a stout pair of gloves, Hamish ventured out into the cold and headed for Dalintober pier.

The town was different in the dark hours just before dawn. The majority of Kinloch's citizens were snuggled in their beds, and there wasn't a soul to be seen. Nothing moved, there were no cars on the road, and the whole place seemed frozen under the great splash of light from a full moon. As Hamish turned a corner, the loch now in view, it cast a great shimmering ribbon across the water. Fishing boats bobbed, a crow shifted from foot to foot on the branch of a tree, its head still under its wing, and a black cat made Hamish jump as it scurried across his path.

He took to the promenade, huddling into his coat against the chill breeze blowing off the loch. The very thought of spending a night out in a tent in such weather seemed akin to madness. But faced with the same difficulties, he couldn't imagine a less dramatic, never mind more effective, course of action. Kinloch could be an unforgiving place to those perceived as wrongdoers, even though what had happened had been little more than an unfortunate accident.

By the time he reached Dalintober pier, it was just before five. He looked about, but there was no sign of Hoynes. Hamish walked along the pier, which once served a separate town. Kinloch had been split in two. But when the head of the loch had been reclaimed, the place became one. Though, even now, there were those who wouldn't live on the north side – and vice versa – not for all the tea in China.

There were three vessels at the pier. Two were fishing boats like the *Girl Maggie*. Just under a ladder sat an open craft, adorned with lobster creels and a pile of old tarpaulins to keep the rain off. Though there was, as yet, no sign of the real thing, the *Golden Dawn* looked in reasonably good shape, given that her owner had fallen out of a taxi some weeks before, following the consumption of a surfeit of whisky, and managed to break his leg.

Hamish stood for a few moments. There was still no sign of Hoynes, so he decided to make his way down the ladder and board the *Golden Dawn*. Once on the vessel, he could at least find some warmth under one of the tarpaulins while waiting for his skipper.

Hamish placed one foot carefully on the side of the boat, before stepping off the ladder and safely aboard. He made his way between some creels before reaching the tarpaulins. Just as he was about to lift one and crawl underneath, the black material stirred and, without warning, a dark figure rose from its midst, sending Hamish staggering backwards.

'Will you stop banging aboot like some bull in a china shop?' said Hoynes. 'Man, you'll wake the whole toon. I've been lying under this bloody tarpaulin for an hour. Come on, let's get underway before everyone's up and aboot.'

With Hoynes choosing to stay partially hidden, it was Hamish's job to fire up the engine, a small in-board diesel.

'That's one hell o' a racket, Hamish,' Hoynes complained as his first mate cast off from the pier.

'There's no' much I can do aboot it, Sandy. Unless you want me to row oot the loch, that is.'

Hoynes stroked his beard. 'Now there's an idea, right enough, Hamish.'

'Well, there's no oars, so you're no' on. I'll keep the revs down, and hopefully that'll keep the racket doon.'

With Hoynes concealed once more under a heap of tarpaulins, they made their way into exile to the chug of the engine. Just as they reached the head of the loch, by the island, a large gull flew low over the boat.

'Look at that great bugger o' a thing, Sandy. Between it and you jumping out the shadows, my heart's going like the clappers.'

'It's a fine beast, right enough, Hamish. Trust me, it's a good sign.' Hoynes watched the great bird soar into the air and head for the hills above Kinloch.

'It'll take us a while to get to Portroy beach. I wish I'd had some breakfast,' said Hamish.

'I thought you'd be light on victuals, what wae your mother still being asleep.' Hoynes handed Hamish a small package wrapped in a brown paper bag. 'Marjorie made them for you. The bacon's cold, but it's welcome at whatever temperature on such a morning.'

Hamish munched down on the bacon sandwich as he navigated between the two buoys that guarded the passage in and out of the loch. Soon, the stars still sparkling overhead, they were in the sound. Hamish turned the vessel north and made for their destination.

'I hope you've got all you need, Sandy. It wouldna be me, camping oot in weather like this.'

'But, remember, you've no' just sunk an expensive vessel belonging to the most vindictive man alive. It's enough to send a soul to the Antipodes wae a view to escape, so it is.'

Now out of the loch, Hoynes felt it was safe to puff a pipe into life. He drew at it lovingly, watching its smoke curl up to the stars. 'Man, we might be on the run, but sometimes it's just good to be alive. Look at the beauty o' it, Hamish.'

But Hamish's gaze wasn't set on the tumble of stars in the clear sky, but on other lights he'd spotted. 'Look, skipper, to starboard, there's a vessel heading this way!'

Hoynes's head snapped round. Sure enough, the lights of an approaching boat were clear in the cold air.

'Do you think it's the fishery officer, Sandy?'

'Don't talk daft, Hamish. He doesna get oot his bed before noon. I hope it's no' the Revenue.' He reached into his pocket and produced a hip flask from which he drew a decent enough dram. 'I'd gie you a swallow, but it's no' the right thing for the man at the tiller.'

'And the sun's no' up yet, never mind o'er the yardarm.'

'I've been under great stress, as you well know. And this isna helping.' Hoynes knocked back another dram and smacked his lips. 'Man, just the thing for this cold weather.'

Though night still reigned over the sound, Hamish had sharp eyes. He peered at the vessel as it neared theirs. 'I'd bet my last penny it's Davie Robertson in the *Sea Harvester*. It's no' like him to be out at this time o' year – or this time o' morning, come to that.'

Hoynes angled his head in the direction of the oncoming craft from under the tarpaulins. 'Worse still, he's the biggest gossip in the toon. If he sees me at this caper, the game's up.'

'Just you stay hidden under there, Sandy. I'll think o' something.'

'I'd like to say I'm convinced of your skills at such matters, but I've little choice.' Complete with his pipe, Hoynes disappeared beneath the tarpaulins.

The chug of the *Sea Harvester*'s engines rent the early

morning air. Her skipper cut them, and she drifted towards the little lobster boat.

'Ahoy there! Is that you, MacEachran?' shouted Robertson from the wheelhouse. The *Sea Harvester*, though a more modern vessel, resembled the *Girl Maggie*, if rather broader in the beam and with generally larger proportions. Having come from the same shipyard, this was no surprise. Robertson never failed to taunt Hoynes about his vessel being the newer, more commodious and of better design.

'It's me, Davie. Hamish from the *Girl Maggie*.'

There were only a few yards between them now. Robertson keened his head out of the wheelhouse. 'It's yourself, right enough. Has Hoynes got you at the boat rustling now?'

'What?' said Hamish, quite confused.

'It's the same as cattle rustling, but wae fishing boats. Man, you're no' yourself this fine morning, Hamish. No' sharp at all.'

'Sandy promised to take auld Willie's boat a run – keep her ticking o'er, so to speak.' The conceit of it all was making the first mate nervous.

'Aye, I see the sense in that. But could you no' do it during the day?'

'I've things to attend to. You know, what wae the *Girl Maggie* being back on the slip.'

'Are they training you how to launch missiles? I've been o'er on Arran playing a couple o' Christmas functions. The whole island is on aboot it. An old boy asked me if Hoynes had any intention of coming to Lochranza. He's planning to go to his sister's in Brodick if your skipper hoves into view. There's folk in fear all up and doon the West Coast, and that's a fact.'

'It was an accident, nothing more.'

Robertson eyed Hamish with suspicion. 'Man, you're jumpy the day, eh? Too much o' the drink?' He gazed at the tarpaulins. 'Or have you something to hide, young fella?'

'What on earth would I have to hide, Davie?'

'Och, when I was a younger man, my father had that wee skiff. She'd been a ring netter, but he kept her for nostalgic reasons. I can tell you, there was no better way to spend some time alone wae a young lady. I'd some good times on that wee boat, I'll tell you.' His face took on a faraway look as he brought to mind past romantic encounters. 'Don't worry, I know fine what Kinloch is like. Everything you do is scrutinised, and that's a fact. Yor secret's safe wae me, Hamish.'

Unfortunately, at that moment, Hoynes, who'd been suppressing a cough for longer than was healthy, could do so no more. Made worse by the pile of filthy tarpaulins under which he was concealed, it was a chesty, unhealthy, hacking noise that issued from his throat, indicative of a regular user of tobacco.

Robertson looked on in surprise. 'Are you sure you should have the lassie oot in this weather, Hamish. Man, that's some cough. Reminds me o' my auld grandfaither, so it does. And he had croup!'

Resigned to the fact that Robertson was now sure there was someone else aboard, Hamish had to think on his feet. 'She's recovering fae the pleurisy, Davie. Had a right bad doze, so she did. The doctor said she should get the morning air.'

Under the tarps, Hoynes was rooting for his first mate, though he was doubtful that the excuse Hamish had come up with held water. He felt the cough reflex kick in and reached for his pipe – the only thing guaranteed to stop the convulsion in its tracks.

Davie Robertson looked down on the *Golden Dawn*'s deck once more as a cloud of blue smoke issued from under them, drifting up in the cool, dark air. The familiar odour of tobacco drifted between the boats. Robertson sniffed at it like a dog. 'Aye, she likes a good shag, that's for sure.'

'I beg your pardon?' said Hamish, balling his fists in anger. 'I'll no' have you speak like that aboot the lassie!'

'Tobacco – she has a fine taste in tobacco. You must have heard it called that. Don't you be getting your knickers in a twist, young man. Anyway, I better be off and leave you to your romancing,' said Davie with a wink. 'Here, her name isn't Sandra, by any chance? Sandra Hoynes, that is.'

'Eh?' said Hamish, but his question was lost in the rumble of the *Sea Harvester*'s engines. Robertson waved a jaunty hand out of the wheelhouse, and in a churn of water was off on his way to Kinloch.

Hoynes waited until the sound of the engines drifted off on the breeze. The coast being clear, he pushed his head up. 'Man, you should try your hand at espionage, Hamish. You have a flair for making folk think what you want them to think.'

'I do? Thanks, Sandy.'

'I'm being sarcastic. There's no' a man or woman alive would have fallen for that parade o' nonsense. I might as well have stood up and shouted, *look, it's me on the run!*'

'Well, you didna help matters by puffing at your pipe and coughing your lungs up. Goodness knows what kind o' lassie Davie thinks I'm knocking aboot wae.'

'Davie knows fine what's afoot. He might no' know why,

but when he gets back to Kinloch, he'll put two and two together. *Is her name Sandra?* Did you no' get that?'

'What will we do?'

'You keep your own counsel, Hamish. We stick to the story, and that's that. Anyhow, knowing your record wae the opposite sex, there're maybe folk willing to believe you're trawling aboot wae a lassie suffering fae chronic bronchitis and a love o' good pipe tobacco. In any event, there's nobody can prove otherwise.'

'If you say so, Sandy.'

'Aye, I do. Come on, let's press on to Portroy beach before the sun's up. My thoughts are wae those poor folk o'er on Arran – fair suffering the dirges Davie comes oot wae on thon banjo o' his, they must be.'

They sailed on: Hoynes deep in thought as to the consequences of their unfortunate encounter with Robertson, Hamish fretting about what his mother would say if she heard tell of the unhealthy woman under the tarpaulin.

13

After a spell of quiet sailing, Hoynes puffing at his pipe as Hamish made sure all was in order with navigation, they happened upon a sandy cove, dotted with rocks.

'This is it, Hamish. Ease her into the sand,' said Hoynes.

Hamish did as he was asked, kissing the *Golden Dawn* to halt on the beach.

'I've taught you well, no doubt about it. I couldna have done that better myself.'

Unused to such praise – any praise – Hamish smiled with satisfaction. He admired his skipper, and to be congratulated for his nautical skills made him proud.

Hoynes looked about, just as the sun, yet to rise, was making its presence felt in the sky. Fewer stars were visible in the firmament, and the moon looked less bright than it had done when they'd left Kinloch. Morning was almost upon the fugitive Sandy Hoynes.

'There's a spot up on the machair that will make a decent place for a tent.' Hoynes produced two ample kit bags, the type used by sailors during the war. 'You take this one, Hamish. There's a couple o' boxes, too. One has food in it, the other has some chopped wood to get a fire going. Stow them on the beach and we'll take things up one by one.'

The fishermen went about their business in a seamanlike fashion, methodically and efficiently. Soon, up on the rough grass, just behind a large rock, Hoynes began pitching the old bell tent.

It was only when they'd laid the groundsheet that Hamish realised how big it was. 'You could fit an army in here, Sandy.'

'I should think so, too, for it came from the army in return for herring. You can fit five in here, at a push.'

This wasn't the discreet hideaway Hamish had imagined. When he picked the next item from the bag, it became obvious that Hoynes had no intention of slumming it in his impromptu camp. 'What's this, Sandy?'

'Man, what a device this is. A wee camping stove, Hamish. It sits inside the tent and fair warms the place up. Aye, and you can cook on her, too. I'll be snug as a bug. The chimney is o'er there – just fit the pieces together, and away we go.'

By the time the tent was assembled, it looked more like something a Bedouin tribesman would call home, rather than a Kinloch fisherman on the run. Hoynes even unfurled a fireside rug, which he spread out in front of the stove. There were two stout camping chairs and a little cot, likely courtesy of the army. Hoynes spread a pile of thick woollen blankets on it and stood back to admire his handiwork, all illuminated under the warm flickering light of an old oil lamp.

'No' bad at all, eh?'

'It'll be cosier when you get the fire going, Sandy.'

'It will that. But I can handle that myself. I want you to come and restock me with supplies and wood every couple o' days, Hamish.'

'How long do you plan to hide out here?'

'As long as it takes Campbell to sort things out. He told me it would take a few days.'

'You're surely no' considering spending Christmas and New Year here?'

Hoynes stroked his beard. 'Well, you could spend it in worse places. Aye, and the cost o' presents alone justifies the inconvenience. No' to mention all these buggers that descend on the hoose at Hogmanay and decimate my whisky. No, things could be worse.'

'What about your wife?'

'Aye, I'll need to clean and cook for myself. But I couldna expect her to suffer such hardship at this time of year.'

'No. I meant, she'll be fair lonely. You know, you hiding out and her all alone o'er the festive season.'

'Och, she'll be fine. Marjorie is great at amusing herself. She'll likely get the cards oot and play some solitaire. Aye, and there's always the wireless.'

Hamish looked at him doubtfully. 'It doesna sound like much fun to me, Sandy.'

'You're a young man, Hamish. Excitable. It's all drugs and the free love to you. For people oor age, well, we'd rather have a good bowl o' cock-a-leekie soup. Here, have a dram and stop your havering.' Hoynes reached under the covers of his cot and produced a bottle of whisky.

'I'll have one – just to banish the cold, you understand. Mind, I've got to get Willie's boat back to Kinloch, Sandy.'

'A true lifeline, so it is. Don't forget – come back the day after tomorrow, same time. Aye, and bring any news o' Campbell the lawyer and bloody Dreich.'

'No' this early, surely?'

'Most definitely! The fewer folk see you going aboot

your business, the better. And don't worry about Davie Robertson. He canna prove that wisna your young squeeze under that tarpaulin.' He sipped his dram. 'Hopefully, Campbell will come up wae something and I'll be home in no time. But meantime, Willie MacEachran's boat is pivotal to the operation. Man, I've never seen a man fonder o' a vessel. It's breaking his heart that he canna get aboard wae that leg in plaster. It's a credit to us that we're trusted wae the thing.'

Hamish finished his dram, feeling its warmth in his chest. It was cold, but he was sure that once Hoynes got the fire raised, things would warm up.

'Right, you get back to Kinloch, Hamish. Take a wee trip up to see Campbell. He's expecting you. He'll give you all the latest on my legal difficulties. Keep your ear to the ground and make sure to rubbish anything that bugger Robertson has to say. Come on, I'll walk you back down to the boat.'

They left the tent and stepped back into the morning. The sun was now above the horizon, though the moon still loomed large in the sky. A patch of stars still shone in the part of the heavens yet to be liberated by light. The sound was still, not a wave to be seen, its surface like glass.

Hamish was first on the beach. But the sight that met him sent his heart into his mouth. 'Oh dear!'

'What are you *oh dear*-ing aboot, eh?' Hoynes followed Hamish's gaze. There was one vessel to be seen, bobbing as though at anchor about five hundred yards from the shore. Normally, this wouldn't have been worthy of a mention. But the fact that the craft in question was the *Golden Dawn* saw Hamish's jaw drop and the pipe slip from Hoynes's mouth.

'I thought you put her at anchor, Sandy.'

'You were skippering the barky. It was your job to make sure she was secure!'

'I suppose I'm used to you giving me the order.'

Hoynes shook his head. 'Here was me praising your skills as a mariner when you kissed the beach, while all the time I'd have been as well having Marjorie at the helm.'

Hamish threw off his pea jacket and began pulling his jumper over his head.

'What on earth are you doing?' said Hoynes, liberating his pipe from the sand.

'She's no' that far oot. I can swim to her and get her back to the shore.'

Hoynes clamped his hand on Hamish's shoulder. 'Man, don't be daft. That water will freeze you solid. It's bad enough having Dreich on my back, without having your death on my conscience into the bargain.'

Hamish pulled his jumper back down. 'Thanks, Sandy, I appreciate it. I'm so sorry aboot the boat.'

'Don't get carried away. At the moment I'm swithering as to whether to ram this pipe doon your throat or not. How could you have been so careless? That's us lost two boats in a matter o' days. Back to the tent. Aye, and you better get used to it, for we'll likely be here for the rest o' oor lives. Forget the legal consequences, the shame will keep us here for ever.'

Hamish looked on as Hoynes stomped back up the beach to the campsite. There had been many moments in his life he'd been happy to forget. This was, undoubtedly, one of them.

14

By lunchtime, Kinloch was awash with gossip. Not only had Willie MacEachran's boat disappeared from Dalintober pier, neither Sandy Hoynes nor Hamish were anywhere to be seen.

Peeny stood at the bar of the County Hotel, a mug of tea in front of him rather than a dram. When Malcolm Connelly appeared through the door, he eyed this spectacle quizzically.

'Have you taken the pledge, Peeny?'

'No, that I have not, Malcolm. You'll have heard the stories about Sandy and Hamish?'

'I know they've gone. You want to hear Galbraith doon at the slip. He swears that Hoynes has decamped so he doesna have to pay the repair bill.'

'Och, his backside. The man must take some o' the responsibility in all this. After all, it was him that made the repair.'

'And it was the repair that shot oot the hatch and sank Dreich's boat. You're right enough. You know Sandy as well as I do. He'll be up to something.'

Peeny stroked his chin. 'Based upon previous experience, you'd think so. But I'm no' so sure. Remember, the man's no' been the same since Dreich appeared back in the toon. He took to his bed for nearly a fortnight. They tell me Marjorie had to get Hamish to pull him from under the sheets and drag him into a bath. Fair stinking, he was. Aye, hair straggling doon his back and a beard like an oak tree in full leaf.'

'Away! I canna believe that, Peeny. He didna look any different to me the other day.'

'He'd put things to rights by that time. I'm telling you, I saw a change in him.'

'Is that why you're on the tea?'

'No, my wife's away to get my pension. That miserable bugger behind the bar wouldna advance me the price o' a dram.'

'I'll sort you oot wae that, man.'

'Very kind o' you, Malcolm.'

'When will she be back?'

'Who?'

'Your wife wae the pension.'

'Just directly, I reckon.'

'Great, you can pay me back when she arrives.'

Peeny eyed his old friend. He was famous for his parsimony, and it was clear that nothing had changed.

With their drams, they took a seat at the back of the bar to discuss Hoynes's plight.

'I think it's time for us to stand up and be counted, Malcolm,' said Peeny. 'We all know fine what a rascal Sandy can be. But there's no' one o' us he hasn't helped o'er the years.'

'Aye, he kept my boat going when I'd the mumps thon time.'

'And he ran my Janice up and doon to Glasgow when I had to get my appendix oot.'

'No' forgetting the time he bailed us oot the jail on Islay.'

Peeny winced. The infamous Battle of Bowmore was still

talked about. The Kinloch football team had been on the island to play their Islay counterparts. Unfortunately, following an away victory, things got out of hand, and the Kinloch contingent, holed up in a bar in the centre of the town, did a fine job of defending themselves against angry locals.

'Man, that was a day and a half. Hard to think it's o'er thirty years ago.'

'Och, the weans these days are too soft to do the game justice, Peeny. They all want to be George Best. Mair interested in strong drink and women than they are in football.'

The pair took a gulp of their drams in unison.

'The drink, if you canna handle it, it's a curse, right enough. Best is throwing away his talent, and that's a fact,' said Peeny.

The door swung open, revealing a bleary-eyed Davie Robertson.

'You've no' got that banjo wae you, I hope?' said Connelly.

'I've had enough o' that for a while. I played two Christmas parties on Arran. My fingers need a rest.'

'We should be thankful for small mercies,' said Peeny. 'We're discussing Sandy and Hamish. Nowhere to be found, apparently.'

'I saw them this morning. Well, Hamish was at the tiller o' Willie MacEachran's lobster boat, and Sandy was hiding under a pile o' auld tarpaulins. Hamish tried to make out he was on a mission wae some lassie. But she must smoke the same baccy as Hoynes, and besides that, she has one hell o' a smokers' cough.'

'Where were they headed?' asked Peeny.

'It was top secret, wherever it was. Hamish wisna for saying, and Sandy was staying put, playing deid. The pair o' them must think I'm half daft.'

Peeny smiled. 'Nobody can say you're half daft, Davie. You canna sing, and you get a terrible racket oot o' that banjo, but you're no' daft.'

Davie Robertson was about to protest when once more the door was flung open.

Peeny's wife Janice rushed into the bar. 'Thank the Lord you're still here. I came as quick as I could.'

'Man, you're desperate for your pension, right enough,' said Connelly.

'What's the matter, Janice?' said Peeny. 'You're as white as a sheet.'

'They found auld Willie MacEachran's boat in the sound about an hour ago. Just fair floating like the *Mary Celeste*, so she was. The daft bugger likely tried to take her oot wae that broken leg and got into difficulties. Poor old soul. He fair loved that boat.'

Peeny gave Davie Robertson a knowing look. 'It's no' Willie we have to be worried aboot, is it, Davie?'

'What are you three at?' said Janice, looking between them.

'It's a long story, dear. Suffice it to say, I think we should get ourselves doon the pier and speak to Mitchell the harbour master.'

'Aye, you're right.' Connelly nodded in agreement. 'I'm thinking this whole episode sounds wrong. Maybe the accident, and all that's happened since, has sent Sandy oot his mind.'

'To be fair,' said Robertson, 'considering the amount o' whisky he can put away, he was rarely in it.'

'Kidding and swanking aside, he's oor pal, has been all oor lives. And Hamish isna much mair than a boy – despite the way his hair's retreating at a rate of knots,' said Connelly. He looked at Peeny. 'You better let herself gie you that pension. Mind, you still owe me the price o' a dram.'

'That's the spirit, Malcolm. Poor Sandy and Hamish have maybe drawn their last breaths, and all you can think aboot is money. Gie him two shillings, Janice,' said Peeny.

'Oh, I forgot all aboot your pension. You'll need to queue up at the Post Office and get it yourself. I've folk to tell as to the truth o' this matter.' Janice got to her feet, and before her husband had time to protest, she was off at a clip to keep Kinloch informed.

'What were you saying aboot money, Peeny?' said Connelly.

'The pension can wait. Let's get down and tell Mitchell what Davie witnessed. I'm thinking we need to rally round. There's no' a man or boy in the fleet who won't sail out for Hoynes.'

15

On Portroy beach the mood was one of despondency. Hoynes was sitting on the camping cot drawing on his pipe thoughtfully, while Hamish whittled away with his penknife at a piece of wood he'd found on the shore.

'I think this looks like one o' they moon rockets they keep talking aboot,' said Hamish, admiring his own handiwork.

'You've some imagination, right enough. No common sense, but plenty imagination.'

Hamish threw the little piece of wood to the ground. 'I'm going for a walk. It would pay you to remember that you were the one who conceived this ridiculous plan. If you ask me – and I hate to say it – but you're just avoiding your responsibilities.'

Hoynes eyed his first mate with disdain. 'You should have been there to advise me, Hamish. You know how carried away I get when it comes to Dreich MacCallum. You should have been there to talk me doon, and no' had me racing oot onto the loch like some madman. Any engine repair must be treated wae respect.'

'So it's my fault! That's it, I'm off!' Hamish pulled his cap down on his head and ducked out of the tent.

Hoynes shook his head. He knew that the entire predicament was down to his foolhardiness. Normally, he was a man of quiet calculation, who weighed up his options and the likelihood that his plans – not always entirely legitimate – were achievable. MacCallum's presence seemed to have robbed him of this innate sensibility. He left the tent and wandered down the beach to the water's edge.

Like most men of his profession, Hoynes could observe the sky, feel the wind on his face, sniff the air and be able to foretell the weather. As he stood, he saw the Isle of Arran obscured by pearlescent cloud. The breeze – already cold – carried the promise of something more visceral, a chill that would work its way through to the bones and remain there until the weather changed. It was going to snow.

'Damn me!' he cursed to himself. 'If it's no' one thing, it's the next.'

Hoynes heard the cry of a bird and looked up. High above, a great gull was circling. Silhouetted by the low winter sun, it looked like a crucifix in the sky, its long wings outstretched as it rode the wind.

'I'd love to be as free as you,' he whispered to himself as he gazed at the seabird. He thought back to being young, with few cares and worries. Time and tide were odd things. The older he became, the more he felt the cold of winter and the heat of summer. The rain made his joints ache, and no number of jumpers and jackets could keep out the chill of frost and snow.

'But you can be free.'

Hoynes looked round. The beach was deserted, save for a seal lumbering into the sea a few yards away and the bird that still hovered in the fading yellow of the sun.

'Everyone will be free one day of the cares that hold them down.'

As he gazed across the sound again, the sky seemed to change. The pearlescence remained, but it took on a darker, purple hew.

'Sometimes you have to let go, Sandy.'

Though he knew the voice was in his head, it was distinct, familiar, not some stray thought or fancy.

'Hona, is that you?'

The question was greeted with silence.

It was as though the world had stopped turning. Nothing moved. The seal had disappeared, and instead of the gull circling in the sky, it hung there, motionless, in quiet benediction.

'Is it my time?' said Hoynes.

'No, not yet. But one day it will be. It will be here, in this place.'

The words should have shocked the old fisherman, but instead they were strangely comforting.

'Everyone must face the end with as much strength as they can muster. It's fear of the unknown that makes us scared to face this day. But there need be no such emotion. In life, we all have purpose, no matter how small or insignificant that may seem. In the end, the meek and the mighty, the weak and the strong are as one. And there is peace.'

Hoynes closed his eyes. It would be so easy to let go. The thought had crossed his mind during his self-imposed exile in bed.

'You don't want to lose those you love. But love can never be lost, not ever. It stays in your heart for eternity, as do all you care for.'

'But what about your enemies? They have a knack of appearing just when you don't expect them.'

'Friend, foe – what does it really mean? A lifetime spent

slaying demons leaves only the shell of a man who is intimately acquainted with those things. Seek out not those who make you happy, but those you love.'

'Aye, makes sense, I daresay.'

Laughter echoed in Hoynes's head. 'Of course it makes sense. Why on earth would you want to be with those who drag you into the depths? For you, the time will be slow. But for me – well, it will happen in an instant. I will see you soon, my friend.'

In a split second, it was as though the world sparked back into life. The breeze was fresh on his face, birds called in the grey sky, and he saw the distant hull of a ship somewhere off the Ayrshire coast. As he made his way back up the beach, he was deep in thought. Flakes of snow landed on his jacket and settled there, white and sparkling.

Did he fear death – the end? Yes, any sane person would. But somehow, Hona's voice in his head had allayed those fears. After all, this man, this entity – whatever it was – must come from somewhere.

Could Hona be a figment of his own imagination? Did the man that so fascinated him only exist in his mind?

But that couldn't be. After all, he'd escaped many problems – near death, even – thanks to his distant ancestor. He'd seen the man before he read about him in a book. He seemed as real as any creature – maybe more so. Nature, red in tooth and claw, as he'd heard said.

'There are more things in heaven and earth,' he whispered to himself.

As he made his way back to the tent, Hoynes was aware that time had passed. The sun was in a different place in the sky. He puzzled on this as he ducked back into the bell tent.

'Where on earth have you been, Sandy? I was beginning to get worried,' said Hamish.

'I was only down at the shore.'

'Which shore? When you didn't appear back, I took a wander down, and there was no sign o' you. Man, you must have been gone for o'er three hours.'

'Away and stop your havering, man.' He looked back out of the tent flap. It was snowing heavily now. They'd need to find more wood to burn.

'How do you like this, Sandy?' Hamish was holding up the top branches of a small fir tree. 'I reckoned that if we're to be here over Christmas, we'd best have a tree. I found these pine cones – they'll do as decorations.'

Hoynes looked at the tree, then back at his first mate. 'Can I ask you a question, Hamish?'

'Aye, of course.'

'Do you believe in something different – you know, otherworldly, that sort o' thing?'

'I know I've had feelings about things before they happen. You know that.'

'I do. Well, pour yourself a drink and sit by that fire, for I've a tale to tell.'

16

Dreich MacCallum watched his wife as she brushed her hair in the mirror. She was a beautiful woman, of that there was no doubt. Kind, gentle, affectionate, Tabitha was everything he could have wished for and more than he deserved. But she'd been brought up in the bosom of a privileged family. Many would have put her outlook on life down to being a spoilt only child. But, as he'd discovered, the woman he'd met as a young captain of a small charter vessel just assumed that life was filled with nice things. And despite himself, he couldn't hold it against her.

'Oh, James, I'm so angry about the boat. You sailed her all the way here and this happens. Rotten luck, if you ask me.' Tabitha applied a touch of rouge to her cheeks.

'I know, bloody bad luck. I couldn't wait to take you out in her and show you where I'm from.' Dreich was shuffling through some papers that he'd spread across the bed. He picked one up, sighed and tucked it into the breast pocket of his jacket.

'What does one eat in Kinloch? Fish, I suppose,' said Tabitha.

'You'd be amazed, Tabby. I saw a man eating a beef sandwich the other day,' he said sarcastically.

She stared back at him, not sure if he was being genuine. 'Don't be mean, James. I'm starving.'

'Well, once you're ready, we'll go for lunch.'

Tabitha checked her reflection in the mirror and smiled. 'All set.'

Locking the room door behind them, the MacCallums made their way down to the spacious dining room. They took a seat under a tall window with panes of stained glass, through which diffused an amber light that spilled onto the white linen tablecloth.

'Now, let's see if your tales about beef sandwiches are on the money.' Tabitha picked up a lunch menu from the table.

As she was taking it in, a young waitress appeared. 'Good afternoon to you. I have a message for you, Mr MacCallum.'

'Oh yes, who from? Hoynes, I hope.'

'No, it's from Mr Campbell the lawyer. He's waiting in the lobby. Just arrived.'

Dreich had been waiting for a meeting with someone representing Hoynes. This was his chance. The man could run, but he couldn't hide. 'I'll be with him directly, thank you.'

The waitress left, and Tabitha turned to her husband. 'I thought we were having lunch together, darling?'

'And we are. I'll only be a few minutes with this Campbell chap. He'll be pleading poverty on Hoynes's behalf, I'm sure.'

'Oh dear. I mean, it's such bad luck. But this fisherman chap, how can he afford to pay you back?'

'He has a boat of his own, dear. Get yourself a G&T, and I'll be back in a jiffy.'

In the lobby, an old man in a suit that had seen better days was sitting at a table on his own, a cup of coffee and ream of papers before him.

'You'll be Mr Campbell,' said Dreich, holding out his hand.

'Aye, that I am.' Campbell struggled to his feet and shook Dreich's hand firmly. 'It's a pleasure to see you again, Captain MacCallum.'

'Again?' Dreich studied the man before him. He was overweight, with a stained tie and suit collar spotted in grey ash. He had no recollection of Campbell at all. But he supposed that people changed over nearly half a century.

They took their seats.

'I remember you as a young lad. Your late father, too, God rest his soul.'

'He was a fine man,' said Dreich.

'He was,' said Campbell, not entirely convincingly.

Irritated by this, Dreich bridled. 'I'm having lunch with my wife. Couldn't we have arranged a more convenient time for this meeting?'

'I'll not keep you a moment, I promise, Captain MacCallum. I just have a couple of questions – from Mr Hoynes's insurance company, you understand.'

'I see. To be perfectly honest with you, I'm surprised he has insurance.'

'Mr Hoynes is a stickler for the rule book, I can tell you.'

'That's a bigger shock.'

Campbell donned a pair of half-moon spectacles. 'You sailed to Kinloch from Glasgow before tying up at the pier, am I right?'

'I did. The cruiser was in dry dock for repairs. That yard in Glasgow was where she was originally built, Mr Campbell.' Dreich shifted uncomfortably in his chair.

'That would be Marshall and Sons, Boat Builders. Just off Anderston Quay?'

'Yes, that's correct.'

'Excellent. Now, you work as a ship's captain with the Wiston Steam Packet Company, I think I'm right in saying?'

Dreich nodded.

'Sailing from Southampton?'

'Yes! What is this, twenty questions?'

'Och, I'm just compiling the facts, nothing more.'

'Please be a bit quicker about it.'

'Just so, Captain MacCallum, just so. In that case, let me express my sympathies. It's never easy to lose one's employment.'

'I beg your pardon?'

'I'm sorry. I was under the impression that you were made redundant in September. Is that incorrect?'

'Semi-retirement. I want more time to spend with my wife and children. But I'm still sailing, I assure you. I don't know where you get your information, Mr Campbell.'

'From a Mr Stones. I believe he's the man in charge of personnel at Wiston's. Or am I again mistaken?' Campbell removed a large cigar from the breast pocket of his jacket. 'You don't mind if I smoke, do you?'

Dreich waved his hand. 'Do what you like.'

As Campbell lit his cigar, Dreich fidgeted with his tie. 'Mr Stones isn't the most reliable of men. He's old and has a memory to match. If you're finished, I'd like to get back to my wife and lunch, if you don't mind.'

'Absolutely. I thank you so much for your time, Captain.' Campbell paused. 'Although . . . is that title still appropriate now you're on the beach, so to speak?'

'I'll ignore that. I realise you're only trying to goad me. For the last time, I'm only semi-retired!' Dreich stood, ready to leave.

'Just one final question, if you don't mind.'

'What?' Dreich's irritation was plain.

'If I could have the address of your insurers, please? Just following procedure, I'm sure you understand.'

'I'll have their card sent to your place of business, Mr Campbell. But I think you'd spend your time more profitably working out how to defend your client. Though I doubt you have the wherewithal. Now, if you'll excuse me.' Dreich strode off in the direction of the dining room.

Campbell puffed on his cigar. 'Aye, a bad lot, the MacCallums. Just like his father before him.' He brushed ash from his lapel.

17

The situation at the quay was fraught. Mitchell, though responsible for the harbour, and even the launching of the lifeboat, had no jurisdiction beyond that point. The Coastguard, anxious to discourage a parade of vessels unsuited to the hazards of winter sailing from piling out of port to look for Hoynes, refused to authorise an official search. In any event, heavy snow was already falling in the sound and forecast to reach Kinloch soon. Instead, the local lifeboat and its counterpart from Brodick would search for the missing mariners, so long as conditions permitted.

Malcolm Connelly glared at Mitchell. 'You'll have those men's lives on your conscience. How can you be part of such a thing?'

'You know very well that I have absolutely no authority in this case. The three of you must know what will happen. Folk will be taking off in pleasure craft and all sorts if they hear there's an official search on for Hoynes – and you're more than aware of the sea at this time of year. It's already blizzard conditions further up the coast.'

Peeny looked heavenward, just as the first fat flakes of snow began to fall. 'And if this gets worse, the lifeboats will be called back to port because o' visibility. These men could die o' cold, even if they have managed to reach safety onshore.'

'And they'll be in no condition to seek aid on land,' said Robertson. 'Cold, starving. I widna like to be you having this to think o' as you sit doon wae your goose, Mitchell.'

The harbour master, knowing full well what the consequences of the Coastguard's decision were, lit a cigarette, a slight tremble in his hands. 'There's nothing I can do, and you know it.' He took a puff. 'But I can suggest *something*.'

'Like what?' said Peeny.

'Well, there's nothing to stop you leaving the harbour. I can't stop you, that's for sure. Neither can the Coastguard.'

Peeny caught Robertson's eye. 'Right, Davie. Are you up for it?'

Robertson nodded. 'I was thinking the very same thing myself, Peeny. And there's no time like the present.'

'I'll come too,' said Connelly. 'Have you supplies aboard, Davie?'

'Are you kidding? I came back wae pies, Christmas cake, two geese and a partridge.'

'Are they all in a pear tree?' said Peeny.

'No, and there's nae French hens, neither.'

'I'll just pretend I never heard this conversation,' said Mitchell, turning to head back to his office.

'Will we go now or round up some more fishing boats?' said Connelly.

'You know folk at this time o' year, Malcom. They'll either be half cut or away somewhere. We could rouse a few, but it would take a while.'

'You're right, Peeny. It's best we just get out there before this snow sets in proper.'

'Don't worry, if we get stuck and forced to heave-to, I've got the banjo on board. We can have a singsong.'

Peeny glared at him. 'We already have two missing colleagues. It would be a tragedy to make it three.'

'You men are sore on me. I'll have you know my playing is admired all the way up the West Coast.'

'Please add "and beyond", for that's what we're hoping for.'

'Right, come on, boys. Time's pushing on – let's dae the same.'

Before long, the *Sea Harvester* was chugging out of the loch, as snow fell with evermore determination.

Mitchell watched them until they passed the island at the head of the loch and disappeared from sight. 'Aye, godspeed to you, boys. Bring them back safely.'

✧

Sandy and Hamish had limited success finding wood. The fishermen, unused to life on land, hadn't taken into account that firewood was best when it was dry. In fact, as they'd discovered, when they tried to light some of the branches and twigs they'd scavenged from the woodland above the beach, they sparked and spat, but refused to catch fire.

'Damn me, Hamish. The logs I brought wae me are near done. It'll be a bloody cold night if we canna set light to this wood.'

Hamish looked on with a sigh. Being a man acquainted with the thin places and notions that there may well be something more, beyond the realm of human understanding, he'd listened to Hoynes's tales about Hona the Viking with great interest. But then he began to wonder if the last few weeks had just been too much for his old skipper. The appearance of Dreich MacCallum had changed him, of that there was no doubt. Gone was the man so confident in his own abilities he seemed almost indestructible. The very fact they were holed up in a tent to avoid Dreich as the days turned to Christmas was proof enough of that.

Hoynes stroked his beard. 'It's clear that you'll be a while coming up wae a workable solution, that's for sure.'

'Why would you expect me to know anything aboot this caper? I've never been camping in my life. Well, apart fae a few Scout camps, and they were just up the hill. I could see the hoose fae the tent. And my mother isna fond o' creepy-crawlies. The nearest we ever came to this was going away on my faither's boat and sleeping on it.'

'Hardly an adventure, for sure. When I was a lad, we'd be up the hill every summer. Man, we'd camp under old coats held up wae a stick and eat fish we'd caught roasted o'er a bonfire.'

'Fine in July, Sandy. No' just as easy in December.'

Hoynes, though he wouldn't admit it, had to agree. Many things hadn't gone to plan in his life. But few had ended as disastrously as this predicament promised to. 'We should pile the wood up next to the fire. That way, it might dry off a bit. You be aboot that, while I pour us a dram. Either way, we'll be warmer than we are now, and that's a fact.'

Acknowledging that Hoynes was right, Hamish did as he was asked and piled the paltry collection of broken branches and twigs around the little camping stove. At the moment, it was cosy enough. But it wasn't hard to imagine what would happen when the only wood that would burn ran out.

Hamish took a seat beside Hoynes on the cot. Each of them had an enamel mug containing a decent pour of whisky.

'This reminds me o' a story my faither telt me,' said Hoynes.

'Oh aye, what was it aboot?'

'Wae back, och, in the early eighteen hundreds, three fishermen left the toon. Hale and hearty young men they were. Good lads with promise o' greater things at the fishing, right enough. In fact, one o' them, Donald, was off my mother's side o' the family.'

'They're out at the fishing, so what now?'

'Well, the day wore on, and the weather turned. It had been a middling October morning, but by the afternoon, there were gales, thunder and hailstones. Och, just hellish, all together. As the evening approached, there was no sign o' them.'

'Where were they fishing, Sandy?'

'No' far fae here, as it turns oot. Just out in the sound.'

Hamish automatically looked towards the sound, even though his view was blocked by the flapping canvas of the tent. 'There'd have been a search, eh?'

'No such thing. It was considered too risky. Men wanted tae go, but the womenfolk put paid to that. The young men just had to take their chances.'

'Man, that's a bit rough, is it no'?'

'Hamish, you must understand that things were different then. Life was often short and tragic. Och, we don't know we're living, what wae all oor home comforts and that.'

Hamish looked about the tent. In the flickering light of the gas lamp and the stove, it was hard to see any of the comforts Sandy had mentioned. 'Aye, carry on.'

'As the story goes, nothing was seen o' them for a fortnight or so. They had a service in the Wee Kirk, the lot. The grieving families did their best to carry on, and the whole sad business was relegated to the past.' Hoynes turned to face his first mate, eyes narrowed. 'But as it turned oot, it was far from the end.'

'What?'

Hoynes's voice was low now, almost a whisper. 'On the fifteenth day after they'd disappeared, a farmer oot on his field wae some oxen saw something strange.'

'Oxen? I'm no' sure there were ever many oxen roon here.'

'You're such a pedant, Hamish. Fine, let's forget the oxen. He was oot wae a few coos – does that make you happier?'

'Mair plausible, I think, Sandy.'

'Can I carry on?'

'Of course.'

'Thank you.' Hoynes put the mug to his lips and downed a fair swallow. 'Anyhow, the farmer is oot in a field wae his *coos*, when he sees a man coming towards him. Bedraggled, he was, dressed in filthy clothes – slathered wae blood, so they say.'

'Oh.' Hamish's eyes widened with the excitement of the tale.

'At first the farmer was a bit leery. He didna recognise this fella at all. And you must remember, back then it was worse than it is now. Wae fewer folk aboot, everybody knew every soul on the peninsula. Aye, right doon to the clothes they were wearing that day, I daresay.'

'I find that a bit much, Sandy.'

'You do, do you? Is it a bit like the oxen you couldna get your heid roon?'

'A wee bit, aye.'

'Well, please shut up, or I'll tell you nae mair.'

'Sorry.'

'Right, where was I? Aye, this farmer doesna recognise this

lad fae Adam. But he notices that he's fat, which was unusual in they days.'

'How so?'

'Because there wisna much grub aboot due to the unfortunate lack o' oxen!' Hoynes's lips flattened in displeasure.

'I get the message. I won't interrupt again, Sandy.'

'Good!' He took a puff of his pipe. 'The farmer doesna recognise the lad until he's almost upon him. Then he takes a step back in horror, for this is Donald, one o' the missing lads I'm telling you aboot.'

'The one related to your mother?'

'The very man. Anyway, he approaches the farmer, who asks him where he's been – aye, and how he's turned into a great beefer into the bargain.' Hoynes moved his face a bit nearer Hamish's.

'"You'll need to forgive me," says Donald. "I've done a wicked thing."'

Hamish opened his mouth, about to speak, but Hoynes's warning look was enough to silence him.

'The farmer enquires as to what wicked thing he's done. The lad looks at him, his face taking on this demonic look – pure evil. "We were shipwrecked," says he, quite jocose, so to speak. "We found shelter in an auld cave. But we were beset by a terrible thirst and hunger." The farmer looks at him, but he carries on. "I had to live, I didn't want to die. So I killed the pair o' them, drank their blood and ate them o'er the last couple o' weeks. That's how I've become so fat."'

Hamish shrunk away from his skipper at the horror of it all. 'That's fair disgusting, Sandy.'

'Aye, it is so. But, och, you know folk here. They were having none o' it. They thought Donald had lost his mind.'

'He got off wae it?'

'Well, no' really. He couldna shift the weight and he died o' a coronary in his early forties.'

'Did he eat them or no, Sandy?'

'As I say, folk didna believe him. They assumed that whatever terrible accident had befallen the rest o' the lads had robbed Donald o' his right mind. That was, until fifty years later, when the crew of a fishing boat put in beside the same caves looking for fresh water. One o' the crew took a dander in to have a poke aboot, and there were the remains o' two men, the teeth marks still showing on the bones where the dirty deed had taken place. Donald had been telling the truth all along. He'd eaten his friends to save himself.'

'Good grief!' said Hamish, shaking his head at the in-humanity of it all. 'How did he cook them? He must have managed a fire, Sandy?'

'That's the worst bit. They found no trace o' a fire or of cooked bones. He'd eaten them raw!' He puffed on his pipe thoughtfully. 'Ach, in my opinion, once you go to the lengths o' killing your friends to save yourself, there's nothing a man won't do. So I'm no' that surprised. But it fair scunnered the people o' Kinloch at the time.'

Hamish looked into the dying flames of the camping stove. 'You say this Donald was off your mother's side o' the family?'

'That he was. Though all the time I knew her, I never saw her eat anyone.'

Hamish rushed over to the drying twigs and branches and stoked the fire with them.

18

Marjorie Hoynes was in a state of agitation. Reluctantly, she'd agreed with her husband's plan to escape Dreich MacCallum and his machinations. But when she heard that Willie MacEachran's boat had been found adrift in the sound with no sign of Hamish aboard, panic began to set in.

Thinking on it in her chair beside the fire, she tried to reason everything out. Was there anyone more resourceful than her husband? No. If there was, she certainly hadn't met them. Would he have been forced to adapt the plan to fit prevailing circumstances? Aye, that he would do, if required. So, she reasoned, the fact the lobster boat was found abandoned must be part of a revised plan.

Marjorie made herself more comfortable and decided to catch up with some of the sleep she'd lost since her husband chose to go on the run. All was well, she was sure of it.

Yet when she closed her eyes, dark thoughts began to nag. For a start, if Hamish was with Sandy for some reason, how could they stock up on supplies? The food, water and firewood he'd taken with him wouldn't last long – especially in this weather. What if Sandy had waved his first mate farewell, only for some freak accident to befall Hamish?

Marjorie shook her head in an attempt to clear it of these

harrying thoughts. In truth, though, she felt guilty. She should have gone down to the pier and explained the whole sorry mess to Mitchell the harbour master. But that would only place Sandy in even more trouble.

The whole thing had turned into a nightmare, and one she'd known would transpire as soon as she heard the name Dreich MacCallum. For she was only too well aware of the contempt her husband held for the man, even though he hadn't seen him for so many years. It had become an obsession, verging on madness. In fact, she worried that Sandy rigged the engine on purpose to sink Dreich's boat. But, she assured herself, even her Sandy couldn't construct a missile – could he?

She jumped at the loud knocking at the door. It was official-sounding, like that of a policeman or fishery officer. She wrung her hands as she padded out into the lobby to answer it, fearing the worst. When she opened it, the tall figure before her was picked out against the settling snow by the bright glimmer of streetlights.

'Mrs Hoynes, I hope you don't mind my calling at this time in the evening?'

Though she could hear traces of a Kinloch accent, it had all but been subsumed by an English twang. She stared at him, motionless.

'May I come in? It's a bit chilly out here, and I'd like to have a word with you, if possible.'

Marjorie Hoynes, despite the circumstances, remembered her manners. 'Yes, please come in, Dr— . . . Mr MacCallum.' Though she only remembered Dreich fleetingly from her childhood, it could only be the man himself.

She showed him through to the living room, onto the chair

that was normally occupied by her husband. Instantly regretting this, Marjorie thought about asking him to sit on the couch instead, but she couldn't think of a suitable excuse in time.

'Could I get you some tea, eh, Mr MacCallum?'

'That would be very kind, Mrs Hoynes. White with two sugars, please. Just the thing on a night like this. That snow's getting worse.'

'Yes, it is.' The thought of her husband out in this weather with nothing but an old, moth-eaten tent to keep him warm flashed into her mind.

'Please, call me James. Everyone else does.'

'It's nice to put a face to a name. I don't remember you, I confess. I was only a girl when you left Kinloch.'

'I'm sure you've heard only fine things about me, Marjorie.' Dreich smiled. He watched her bustle off to get the tea, taking his time to look round the room. It was like stepping back in time. A thick rug sat before the roaring fire burning in the stone grate. The wallpaper was a floral chintz pattern, one that would have long been considered passé where he lived. There was a display cabinet containing some crystal vases, silverware and a selection of faded black-and-white photographs. A sideboard sat against the back wall, upon which was a Bush radio – a stout one made in wood veneer, no doubt a relic of the forties. A small television set was positioned in the corner of the room. There was a tiny artificial Christmas tree, with a few festive cards dotted here and there.

Dreich had forgotten how things were in Kinloch. And despite the odd mod con, like the TV and radio, this place reminded him of his mother's front room, from so long ago.

That this brought a lump to his throat surprised him. To fend off this sudden burst of sentimentality, he leaned forward and picked up the copy of the *Kinloch Herald* from the low coffee table before him.

He smiled at the headline: *Dog Toilets To Be Installed in Kinloch*. Just how these facilities were to be discerned by passing dogs puzzled him. He read some more headlines. *Russian Satellite Visible Before Christmas. Frank MacLeod's Sheep Are Champions. Kinloch United Beat Oban Thistle Again.*

He smiled and laid the paper down just as Marjorie appeared with a tray of tea and sweetmeats.

'You shouldn't have gone to so much trouble, Marjorie. Homemade shortbread. Goodness me, I haven't tasted that since I left.'

'Please, help yourself. Made fresh today.' Marjorie sat down opposite her guest.

'I'll not bother you for long. But I have to ask you a question,' said Dreich.

'Oh yes,' she replied, dreading it.

'Marjorie, if you know where your husband is, you should speak out. What happened the other day with my boat must be resolved. Sandy can't just run away from his responsibilities, you know.'

She felt like saying that he'd been doing that since the day they were married, but managed to resist the temptation. 'My husband is away on business.'

'Oh, come on, you can't really believe that.'

'I can and I do.'

'He was spirited off in the middle of the night in a boat that didn't even belong to him. I know you know where he is.'

'Are you calling me a liar, Mr MacCallum?' Marjorie raised her chin. She was from a family that had fished the waters around Kinloch for as long as anyone could remember. She was determined not to let this effete exile call her honesty into question.

Dreich decided to change tack. 'I apologise. But you must see the position this leaves me in. I'm out of pocket. And whoever is to blame for the sinking of my vessel – either your husband or Mr Galbraith – it has to be sorted out.'

'Aye, well, Sandy will deal with it on his return. In the meantime, Mr Campbell the lawyer is looking after the matter on his behalf. I'm sure he'll be more than happy to help you.'

Dreich forced a smile and looked uncomfortable. 'Yes, I've already spoken to him.'

'So I believe. He tells me you were made redundant. I'm sorry to hear that.' Though Marjorie's face was all sympathy, she felt nothing but disdain for this man. Who did he think he was, coming into her home and casting aspersions on her husband?

'I'm semi-retired, Mrs Hoynes.' Dreich tried to keep his voice neutral, but it was raised all the same.

'That's a shame. No doubt, you'll have been intending to spend mair time on your wee boat.'

'It wasn't a *wee boat*, Mrs Hoynes! I'd just had her refitted at great cost, and now she's at the bottom of the loch.'

'Aye, but isn't sailing just the most dangerous thing?'

'It is when your husband's about, Mrs Hoynes.'

'You're safe then, as he's away at the moment.' She smiled benignly.

Dreich had had enough. It was infuriating to find that the

wife was every bit as thrawn as the husband. 'Aren't you at all worried for Hamish?'

Marjorie must have let her mask slip, because she noticed a flicker of satisfaction on Dreich's face. 'Sandy knows this coast like the back of his hand – aye, and so does Hamish, come to that.'

'Hmm . . . I remember tales of Hamish's grandfather sitting in the corner of the bar at the County telling stories in return for drams. He knew *that place* like the back of his hand. And from what I hear, his father was worse. You'll forgive me if I've little faith in that family.'

'Hamish is a fine lad, and my husband's a good man. He's never cheated anyone out o' anything. He leaves that to others.' Though she said this with great certainty, Marjorie crossed her fingers, not really sure how many people Sandy had got the better of by fair means or foul.

Dreich shook his head. 'My lawyer arrives tomorrow. If you have no regard for your husband's safety, please be concerned about your own responsibilities, *Marjorie.*'

'Why so?'

'Because I hear you have a full share in the *Girl Maggie*, therefore you are partly responsible for her.'

Marjorie wanted to say that she'd only agreed to that on the advice of her husband. He'd been told that his wife having a share would help with his tax. But this was a new worry, something which she hadn't considered.

Dreich stood. 'I'll bid you goodnight, Mrs Hoynes. But if I were you, I'd have a good think about what you're doing. No need to show me out. Thanks for the shortbread.'

With that, he was gone. She heard the front door close on the latch behind him.

'Sandy, you better have a plan – that's all I'll say,' she whispered to herself before draining her cup of tea. But though she was concerned, in her heart of hearts, she knew the man sufficiently to be sure he'd have something up his sleeve.

19

'I'm damned if I know what to dae now, Hamish,' said Hoynes as he watched the last of the wet wood splutter and die in the little stove. The old tent was getting cold – very cold.

'We could go out and see if we can find any good stuff, Sandy.'

'We couldna find any earlier without snow on the ground. How are we going to do it now there's a blanket o' the stuff? No' to mention that it's pitch-black outside into the bargain.'

'You'll have to give me a couple o' the blankets, Sandy.'

'Can you no' wrap yourself up in that fireside carpet? Man, I'm thinking that will be rare and warm.'

'I don't doubt it. But then I'll be lying on the cold ground. I need some blankets, Sandy. Damn, you must have five!'

Hoynes sighed. 'This reminds me o' the boys in the *Gloria*.'

'Don't tell me – one o' them ate the rest.'

'You see, it's that cynicism that'll get you nowhere, Hamish. It's well known that lassies canna stand that type o' person. Fair recoil, they do.'

'Marjorie seems to have stuck by you well enough. You're the maist cynical person I know, skipper.'

'I'm a realist, Hamish. I'm accustomed to the exigencies of life. Aye, and I've experienced plenty o' them o'er the years.'

'If you don't mind me saying, it's your loose grasp o' reality that's got us here in the first place. I mean, who else would have considered making themselves scarce by slipping away in a tent in December?'

'Everything would have worked fine and dandy if it hadn't been for your neglect o' basic seamanship. You'd have been tucked up wae your teddy, and I'd have been cosied in here with a full complement o' blankets.'

Hamish folded his arms. 'I don't have a teddy.'

'Aye, well, I'll apologise for that. It was an overly harsh thing to say.'

'It's a stuffed donkey, if you must know. My mother gave it to me when I was four.'

'Are you being serious?'

'I am. I put him at the back o' my neck on the cold nights. Better than a hot water bottle, so he is.'

Hoynes took time to light his pipe and consider what his first mate had just revealed. He'd never had stuffed toys when he was a wee boy. He supposed they weren't popular back then. And even if they had been, his mother had always been keen that he wasn't mollycoddled as a child. Like her mother before her, a formidable woman, she was convinced that offspring should grow up aware of the many challenges life had in store. His father was a softer, kinder man. But Hoynes had his mother to thank for the steel in his bones, and his never-say-die attitude. He'd needed that often in his life, not least now.

'Are you going to tell me aboot this *Gloria* or not, Sandy?' Hamish knew when it was time to pour oil on troubled waters. Not that they had much of that left, either.

Hoynes furled himself in an old army blanket. 'It had been

an uncommon cold winter – back in nineteen forty-seven, just after the war. You were no mair than a wean, I'm thinking.'

'I was that.'

'The boys in the *Gloria* volunteered to take supplies to Islay. The ferries had all but stopped because folk couldna get to their work for all the snow blocking roads at Tarbert and the like.'

'I mind making a cracking snowman that year. It was bigger than my uncle Donnie,' said Hamish.

'I daresay. But it has to be noted that Donnie was never the tallest o' men, right enough. A fine fellow he was, but hardly of the Samson variety.'

'Samson who?'

'The biblical strongman! What kind o' religious education have you had, eh? The poor man had terrible problems wae his hairdresser, or some such thing. Can I carry on?'

'Aye, I'm with you now, right enough.'

Hoynes shivered and pulled the blanket tighter about himself. With the fire in the camping stove down to nothing more than a glimmer of embers, the only light came from the guttering gas lantern, hung from the apex of the tent. It cast shadows about the place, spinning and dancing on the canvas walls. 'The brave boys – the skipper was a MacAllister – left the quay, fair stocked wae provisions. They made the sail quite easy, the water being calm. A local spotted them a few miles away fae the island, all looking well. But as they waited in Bowmore, the *Gloria* never appeared.'

'What on earth happened?'

'There were many theories at the time. All of them as far-fetched as the last. But the answer came in nineteen sixty-three.'

'How so?'

'There was a man here called MacNair. He'd been clever at the school and ended up at Glasgow University.'

'Clever, right enough,' said Hamish.

'Oh aye, a heid like a prize turnip. Folk used to remark on the size o' it. But he needed a noggin that big to accommodate those brains o' his.' Hoynes stared into the flames, as though bringing the tale from the core of his very being. 'He was that clever he ended up on the Arctic survey team. Are you aware o' such a body, Hamish?'

'Oh aye,' said Hamish confidently. 'They're the fellas that go and count polar bears, penguins and the like.'

'You're half right, Hamish. Man, if you found a penguin in the Arctic, you'd be the biggest celebrity on the planet. Mair famous than that McCarthy chap you like. Him that sings aboot blackbirds.'

'McCartney! His name's Paul McCartney, Sandy.'

'Just so. Well, maybe if he'd sung more about penguins, you'd be better acquainted wae their natural habitat.'

Hamish rolled his eyes, anxious for Hoynes to get on with his story.

'Anyway, your boy MacNair heads off into the frozen North wae his notebook, pen and a decent pair o' gloves, I shouldna wonder.'

'You'd need decent gloves in those climes, Sandy. No doubt aboot it.'

'He's there for a couple o' weeks when he sees this great iceberg a mile or so away. He gets his binoculars oot and, damn me, he sees something lodged on the top o' it.'

'On top o' the ice?'

'Aye, right there on top o' the ice.' Hoynes puffed on his

pipe pensively. 'He gets the captain o' this icebreaker to sail nearer the thing.'

'He'd no' be happy aboot that. There's much more of an iceberg under the surface, you know, Sandy.'

'Aye, and maybe a couple o' rogue penguins. Perhaps that's why no bugger sees them in the Arctic, eh?'

'There's no need for sarcasm, Sandy.'

'You're a dreadful man for lecturing, Hamish. As if I wouldna know that there's mair o' the iceberg underneath the water than there is above it.' Hoynes glared at him.

'Right, a point well made. How did all this end up?'

'The captain o' the icebreaker took her as near as he dared. They were still a distance off the iceberg, but MacNair had a fine pair o' binoculars. He put them to his eyes, but he couldn't believe the evidence o' them.'

'What on earth?'

'There was a fishing boat perched atop the iceberg.'

'Away!'

'Aye, and that's not all. There was a wee trail o' smoke twirling oot the lum at the wheelhoose.'

'Och, I'm no' believing this.'

'As true as we're sitting here in a tent, that's what happened, I'm telling you.'

'Was it the *Gloria*?'

'Aye, that it was. And there was MacAllister standing at the bow, waving his hands like a wild thing. A great beard straggling doon to his feet.'

'But how did she get there? The boat, I mean.'

'You'll remember what a cold winter it had been in forty-seven. Well, for the first time, icebergs began to form oot in the Atlantic, just off Islay.'

125

'I'm no' sure that's how it happens, Sandy.'

'You wae all that accumulated knowledge, eh. As it turns out, the great thing snagged them, and they were dragged north. They spent years living off the supplies intended for the folk on Islay. But they were found just in time. They were down to a few tins o' rice pudding and no whisky for five years. Can you imagine such a thing, Hamish?'

'No' really, it has to be said.'

'But all three were as fit as fiddles. They say the cold air does wonders for the constitution.'

'As we're aboot to find out tonight.' Hamish lifted his cap and scratched his head. 'It's funny I never heard that story before. Aye, and what happened to them afterwards? I'd know if all three o' them had been in Kinloch.'

'Och, they couldna stay in the toon. Didna get a bit o' peace. People just wanted to hear their tales. Plus, it was too painful, as all their wives, assuming they were deid, had married other men. For the good of all concerned, the three of them moved to Oban.'

'Why Oban?'

'You know fine – the only things they're interested in up there is shinty and the ferry timetables. They were just left to their ain devices.' Hoynes took another triumphant puff of his pipe, another tale well told.

Hamish stared into what remained of the little fire in the camping stove. It was only a spark or two of burning wood now, the glow coming from the accumulated ashes. 'But they had coal and plenty food, Sandy. We have none o' either.'

20

Aboard the *Sea Harvester*, spirits had waned. The snow was still falling, if somewhat lighter in nature.

Peeny stood at the prow, wrapped up in a thick sheepskin jacket. He shook his head at the visibility and walked back to the wheelhouse, where Robertson was strumming his banjo.

'Mitchell was right, Davie,' said Peeny. 'There was no point coming out in this. The deck looks like a winter wonderland. I'll set to wae a shovel shortly and clear the worst o' it.'

'Is Malcolm still below?' said Robertson.

'He is that. You know Connelly. A couple o' slices o' Christmas cake and a dram or two and he's lashed to the mast for a fortnight.'

'Mind you, there's no' much needing done, apart fae clearing the snow.'

'I've a good mind to wake him up and get him at it.'

'Mair bother than it's worth, Peeny. You know fine he'll just moan and groan. I'd be happier doing it myself.'

'Aye, true, very true, Davie.'

They looked out of the wheelhouse windows, all framed in snow.

'I wonder how Hoynes and Hamish are faring, Peeny?'

'I wonder if they're *faring* at all, to be honest.'

'This is Sandy we're talking aboot, mind.'

'There's no' a man alive that can outsmart everyone and everything. The minute I heard that Dreich MacCallum was back in the town, I thought o' Sandy. It's like some kind o' prophecy coming true.'

'I never knew there was any prophecy,' said Robertson.

'I was being metaphorical. I mean, they're like these star-crossed lovers you hear all aboot.'

Robertson narrowed his eyes and stared at Peeny. 'I'm no' too sure what you're driving at, Peeny.'

But Peeny's attention was elsewhere. In his late sixties he may be, but there was nothing wrong with his eyesight. 'Would you look at that, Davie.'

Robertson followed the line described by Peeny's finger. Sure enough, held within a perfect circle of cloud sat the waxing moon, bordered by the dark velvet night beyond. 'She's clearing, Peeny!'

'Aye, that she is. I'm away to wake Malcolm. All hands on deck, if we're to find them!' He hurried below as Robertson placed his banjo back in its case and patted it shut.

Connelly stumbled onto the snowy deck, half asleep. 'What's going on, Davie?'

'She's clearing. Hopefully, we can get some idea where Sandy and Hamish are.'

Connelly searched the sky. It was true: the white snow clouds were beginning to break up, revealing a sprinkle of stars. The moon was reflected in the sound and on the white deck, making the accumulation look almost blue in colour.

'What's up wae you?' asked Robertson.

'She might be clearing, Davie, but oor task is every bit as

difficult now as it was when we started out. We still don't know where they are.'

Robertson nodded his head. The thrill of seeing the night sky had been replaced by grim reality. Though he knew Hamish had sailed this way in the lobster boat, there were a myriad of little coves and outcrops upon which the pair may have sought refuge. Then came the darkest thought of all. One of them would have to scan the calm waters for their bodies.

Peeny arrived back on deck with three steaming mugs of tea. 'This'll wake us up,' he said, as he handed one to Connelly and the other through the wheelhouse window to Robertson.

'What hope have we of finding the pair o' them, eh?' said Connelly. 'It's still dark, the snow's piled high on the shore . . . Och, it's just an awful thing.'

The three of them drank their mugs of tea, deep in thought. The sea was cold enough to kill in a handful of minutes. Parted from their boat in this weather, what chance did Hoynes and his first mate really have? That aside, what calamity had befallen them that forced leaving or, more likely, falling out of the vessel?

'I canna imagine what parted them from Willie's boat,' said Peeny. 'It's snowing, but Hoynes could sail through that, no problem. Plus, there wasn't a mark on her when she was found, so it wasn't a collision.'

'Any manner of catastrophes could have befallen them, Peeny. A man overboard, for instance. Hamish is a clumsy bugger at the best o' times. Sandy would do the decent thing and dive in to save him,' opined Connelly.

'Can I ask you a question, Malcolm?' said Davie.

'Aye.'

'See when you were born, did they whack you wae the

pessimism stick right away or hang on until you were a wee bit older?'

'Look over there,' said Peeny. To the east of the vessel, the coast was emerging from the gloom.

'That's fair enough, Peeny,' said Robertson. 'But they could be anywhere up and doon the length of the peninsula – or beyond.'

'But look above, man!' Sure enough, hanging in the air above the dark coastline was an improbably bright star. It seemed to twinkle red as they looked at it.

'It's no' the Pole Star, anyhow,' said Connelly. 'She'll be up there somewhere.' He pointed high into the sky.

'No, nor Venus or any other planet. Man, I've never seen a star as bright as that in the evening sky.'

Peeny looked between the other two men. 'You don't think – well, yous know the time o' year.'

'You think it's the light fae the Firdale Christmas tree?'

'No! Think aboot it, man.'

Robertson was drumming his fingers on his banjo case. 'Do you think it's a flare, Peeny? Is that what you're saying?'

'Man, you pair must either be heathens or the densest folk that ever lived. What happens every Christmas?'

Connelly was first to reply. 'I get hammered and herself goes to her bed.'

'No, try and think a wee bit mair traditionally.'

'Archie Douglas closes the pub at six. Many a year I've been scunnered by that,' said Robertson.

'Hopeless! Think o' the manger, the newborn baby. Ring any bells?'

'Now you're in the realms o' fantasy, Penny. And apart fae

that, it would spell the end o' Christianity. I mean, nobody's going to believe that Hoynes is some kind o' deity.'

'What aboot Hamish?' said Robertson. 'All that seeing into the future lark. Man, that could be significant.'

'You're going to disappoint a lot o' people at the Wee Kirk, Peeny.'

'Look at it, just hanging there. What else can it be?'

Peeny was right; the star was motionless in the sky, as bright as the Ardnamurchan lighthouse on a stormy night.

'Here's something worth considering, given we don't have any better ideas. I reckon we have a good look closer into shore.'

'You're right, Davie. There's nothing lost by having a look. Man, we're fishermen. Every man and boy o' us is as superstitious as they come. Malcolm, you canna see the turn o' the month without shouting "white rabbit!" seven times in a row. And as for you, Davie, I've never known you to take to the stage without a good half-bottle inside you.'

'That's nothing to dae with superstition, Peeny. I just like a good drink.'

'Even so. Pull her in as near to the shore as you can. We can have a look through that big torch you brought. You know the one wae the spinning red light at the top in case you're marooned wae the car.'

'Who died and made you Admiral o' the Fleet?' said Connelly.

'Oh aye, that's right. We should have chosen you, Malcolm. A man o' decision and swift action. Come on, we've lives to save!'

21

In the tent, things were reaching crisis point. As the skies cleared, so the temperatures plummeted. Reluctantly, Hoynes had given Hamish two old army blankets. Not through altruism exactly, but because he feared his second-in-command may perish if he wasn't offered some kind of protection against the biting cold. The camping stove offered nothing save a feeble glow, its flaming potency long expired.

'You'll be fair basking in warmth now, Hamish,' said Hoynes, who as well as sleeping off the floor in a cot, was wrapped up in three blankets. It was also true to say that his more substantial frame gave him an advantage over Hamish, who was naturally thin and wiry, lacking the fatty protection against the cold Hoynes enjoyed.

'Aye, Sandy. It's like the tropics doon here.' The first mate was shivering as he lay swaddled in the blankets atop the old rug Sandy had recovered from his loft. 'But it's a consolation to know that if I die, you'll likely eat me. Though I advise you to warm me up over a low flame so that I'll defrost.'

'Damn me, I've never heard such histrionics. You should be on the stage.'

'I'm at the last stage o' hypothermia, if that makes you feel better.' Hamish had heard about chattering teeth before, though he hadn't really experienced them. Now, he was enduring that very thing, and amazed that he couldn't stop the constant rattle of tooth on tooth.

'There could be a solution – a partial one, at least,' said Hoynes.

'Which is?'

'You'll have to come and share this cot wae me.'

The statement was enough to stop Hamish's teeth clattering off one another. 'Och, you're okay, Sandy. I'll be fine doon here. There's barely enough room for you in that thing, never mind me.'

'That's the whole idea, man. It's that oor body heat is shared. If you were lost in the Alps wae me, that's just what we'd be doing, right this very minute.'

'What on earth would we be doing in the Alps? It's aboot as far away fae the sea as you can get in Europe.'

'Well, you never thought you'd be here this morning, did you now?'

Hamish had to admit that his skipper had the right of it. And, when Sandy Hoynes was about, the oddest things were likely to happen. So, he supposed that their presence in the Alps could hardly be ruled out. In fact, reviewing his circumstances, perhaps it did make sense to remove himself from the cold ground that seemed to be eating away at any heat his body managed to generate. 'We could try topping and tailing, I suppose, Sandy.'

'Now, Hamish. I know we live in a world where things are mair permissive than they were when I was your age. Aye, and that's likely a good thing for folk, but you canna teach an old dog new tricks. So, whatever inclinations you have, I'm afraid

I don't share them. Though I think nothing less of you for making the proposition.'

'It's nothing like that, Sandy! I mean, I'll lie wae my heid at one end o' the cot, and yours at the other.'

'So I'll be staring into your rotten feet?'

'But this way we'll have a modicum o' privacy.'

Hoynes pondered on the subject of topping and tailing for a moment. 'Can I ask who it was that passed on this piece of advice to you, Hamish?'

'Mrs Green, the minister's wife.'

'Man, you've no shame. Intimate wae the wife of a clergyman! There are depths to you I'm feart to confront, Hamish.'

'Eh? She taught us in the Scouts. What else were you thinking, Sandy?'

'I've always thought she'd the glad eye, if you know what I mean. Forbye that, the Reverend Green must be one of the dullest men I've ever met. I couldna blame the lassie for taking up wae a younger man.'

'I think you might be suffering fae that hypodermia, Sandy.'

'It's *hypothermia*, you dolt. Are you going to come in wae me or not? Because I could fair do wae the warmth o' these blankets back.'

There followed a complicated dance that saw Hoynes lift his legs in the air, while Hamish slid underneath them and tried to find a comfortable position in the camping cot. He twisted and turned, eventually reaching something approaching relief.

'Sandy, you've still got your seaboots on,' said Hamish, faced with a large yellow Wellington boot about an inch from his nose.

'And I should think so, too. The only time a fisherman

should be without his boots is when he's at home in bed wae his wife or being laid oot at Smith's the undertaker.'

'If you say so, Sandy.' Despite his discomfort, Hamish had to agree that it did feel warmer. It had been an exceptionally long day, and he felt fatigue creeping over him. His eyelids fluttered and closed.

✧

Aboard the *Sea Harvester* it was all go. Peeny took Robertson's car lamp and shone it on the shore. The broad beam revealed a beach, rocky in parts, mostly covered in thick snow.

'This could be the place, right enough. I've heard Sandy banging on aboot Portroy beach before,' said Robertson.

'Did he no' come here wae his faither when he was a boy? There's a good trout river no' far away,' said Peeny.

'Look!' Connelly was pointing at the beach. 'See, just above the waterline – footprints!'

'Man, you're right enough. The snow's no' been able to lie so close to the sea. I'll be damned.'

'I'll get the rowing boat. We canna get in any closer than this, and I don't fancy wading out in this cold.'

Soon, the rescue party were afloat on the *Sea Harvester*'s rowing boat, reserved for access to harbours lacking in suitable facilities and jaunts onto beaches like this.

Peeny stared skyward. The star was still visible through the trees. 'I must admit, wae Christmas nearly upon us, and that star up there, well, I'm feeling quite overcome.'

'It's odd, to say the least,' said Connelly.

'I'm telling you, if Hoynes is some kind o' deity, I'm changing my religion,' said Robertson.

'To what?' said Peeny.

'I might as well have a crack at Hinduism. I'm sure they'd have no truck wae Hoynes.'

Peeny shook his head. 'There's things aboot this world we'll never know.'

They rowed the little boat ashore, then slid it up onto the sand out of the freezing seawater and secured it. The little party made their way up the beach and stepped into the snow.

'I'm thinking that if Sandy is here, he'll be having a bloody hard time o' it,' said Peeny. 'It's the coldest I've felt for many a year, and that's no joke.'

Robertson took in his surroundings. 'If you were looking for shelter, you'd surely head into those pine trees?'

Collectively, they looked up past the machair and into the treeline. It was obvious: any man would have sought the protection of the forest, given the circumstances.

Connelly wasn't convinced. 'I'm thinking we're on a fool's errand here. We've followed a star and ended up on this beach. I'm sad to say there's a large part o' me that thinks the pair o' them are much mair likely to be at the bottom o' the sound than up in those trees. It's all wishful thinking, lads.'

'Man, you're the cheeriest bugger that ever walked,' said Peeny, glaring at his companion. 'For good or ill, we're here now, so we might just as well have a poke aboot.' He began to trudge up the beach.

✧

'I'm no' sure this is a good idea, Hamish,' said Hoynes. 'I mean, I'm warm enough, but I canna move, and I've got that tingling in my left foot that doesna bode well. No, not at all.'

'What's going to happen to it – spontaneous combustion?'

'The tingling is a harbinger o' cramp. And I tell you, Hamish, I fair dread the sensation. The pain's unbearable. My legs shoot aboot all over the place of their own accord – and that's a fact.'

Hamish stared at Hoynes's yellow boot once more. 'Well, try and give me some warning, at least, so I can remove my face and no' get booted to death. But, mind you, I'm no' going back on the floor o' this tent for love nor money.'

'In that case, be prepared. That's all I'm saying.'

They lay still for a few moments, a wave of tiredness drifting over Hamish yet again. But just as he felt himself drifting into sleep, he was jolted into wakefulness by a sudden flinch from Hoynes.

'I feel the cramp coming on, Hamish!' yelled Sandy.

'Wait and I'll get oot.' Hamish tried to push himself free of the camping cot. But as he did, Hoynes's nearest leg described an arc in the air and pinned him down by the neck with some force. 'Sandy, you're choking me!' he squealed.

The sound that came from Hoynes was akin to that of a boiler about to explode. It began as a deep rumble in his chest, then manifested itself in strangled cries in his throat. As the cramp took hold in pulses of agony, his cries of pain syncopated to it, Hamish's whimpers acted as a counterpoint.

✧

'Did you hear that?' said Peeny, stopping in his tracks in the snow.

'It sounds like some kind o' animal,' said Robertson.

'It'll be rutting stags,' said Connelly. 'They go through a

right performance when they're at the rutting.'

Not listening at all, Peeny hurried ahead with the lamp, the other two close on his heels.

'Look, there's a tent behind that rock!' Peeny shouted amidst the yells and moans coming from inside.

'We better get in there, quick smart,' said Robertson. 'It sounds like murder.'

They made for the tent. Peeny stopped and wrenched the tent flap open, sending a button spinning into the cold night air, then shone the torch inside. Robertson and Connelly looked over his shoulder.

Illuminated by the beam of light, the sight that met their eyes was hard to describe. One yellow Wellington boot was thrust in the air. In the crook of the other leg, Hamish's face, contorted with pain, was visible as he screeched and moaned. At the opposite end of the cot, Sandy Hoynes's head was thrown back in the excruciating agony of cramp. The sound that issued from his mouth approximated the first paroxysms of someone about to sneeze, though much more voluble.

'In the name o' the wee man!' Peeny exclaimed, staring at the writhing tumble of legs, arms, heads and blankets, his mouth agape.

'We should let them have their privacy,' wailed Connelly above the racket.

Hamish's eyes shot open. 'Get him off me!'

As one, the three fishermen were galvanised by this cry for help. At first, Peeny and Robertson tried to prise Hamish's head from the tight grip of Hoynes's leg. But this proved more difficult than first anticipated, as the older man's limb seemed set like steel.

'Sandy, you're choking Hamish to death. Move your leg, man!' Robertson shouted.

'I canna help myself,' said Hoynes through his pain.

'In that case, just pull yourself together, man. I'm no' sure what's got into you, but now's the time to stop it. No wonder the pair o' you came a way oot here in a tent. I've never seen the like,' said Peeny.

There was something in the undertone of what his old friend said that afforded Hoynes a brief respite from the crippling cramp he was experiencing. He managed to move his leg enough to free Hamish's head. The first mate shot from the cot like a bullet and landed on the hard ground. Meanwhile, Hoynes's release from pain was a brief one. His leg shot into the air again, catching Connelly square on the nose. The latter fell back, blood pouring down his face.

'Hamish, how are you?' said Peeny. 'What's got into your skipper? You don't have to tell me if you don't want to, son.'

'He's got cramp. Pull his legs straight and it should give him some relief, Peeny,' said Hamish amid the commotion.

'Aye, I've heard it called that, right enough.' But, doing as Hamish had asked, he and Robertson grabbed a leg each, almost pulling Hoynes off the cot.

'Oh, that's better,' said Hoynes, the cramp beginning to ease.

'Speak for yourself,' Connelly groaned as blood from his nose dripped through his cradling fingers.

22

It took two trips to get them back aboard the *Sea Harvester*. Hoynes insisted on bringing back certain items, including three bottles of whisky, the little stove and the cot. The tent, it was decided, had seen better days and was as well left where it was.

Peeny sat with Hamish and Hoynes, as they warmed up below with hot tea.

'Now, there's no need to explain yourselves, lads. It's nineteen sixty-eight, and folk have the right to let it all hang oot if they want.'

'What does he mean, Sandy?'

'He's trying to imply that you and I were involved in biblical congress when they arrived in the tent.'

'We should have prayed, right enough,' said Hamish seriously. 'But, och, it just all happened so quickly, didn't it?'

Peeny looked between the pair as though he was seeing them for the first time. 'So, you were kind o' caught up in the whole . . . moment?'

'I had cramp! Plain and simple, Peeny.'

'And why was Hamish in there wae you?'

'We were topping and tailing, Peeny. Mrs Green the

minister's wife taught me how to do it when I was in the Scouts,' said Hamish.

Peeny, who had just taken a gulp of tea, now proceeded to spray it everywhere.

'Hamish was freezing to death wrapped up in my fireside rug. We had to huddle together for warmth, plain and simple. Shared body heat, man! Now, enough o' your innuendo. Aye, and you can tell your pals up in the wheelhouse the same thing,' said Hoynes.

Peeny decided to change the subject. 'We followed a star, you know.'

'Like in the Bible?' said Hamish.

'Aye, that's how we found you. I'm no' telling a word o' a lie, son.'

'What do you make o' that, Sandy?'

'There must be a desperate shortage o' Wise Men, if you ask me.'

Ignoring this, Peeny continued. 'We'll be back in Kinloch before you know it, Sandy.'

'As long as it's still dark, I'm no' bothered.'

'Why dark, skipper?' Hamish asked.

'Because Dreich MacCallum's still on my tail, that's how. That's why we were where we were – or had you forgotten?'

'Aye, of course.'

'You'll just have to face him, Sandy,' said Peeny.

'I'd rather have a few hours in bed and a good cooked breakfast before I do. So, you can keep this quiet until later.'

'But Davie's had to call the harbour master. The lifeboat was oot looking for you. We canna have folk risking life and limb just to keep you fae Dreich,' said Peeny.

Hoynes made a face and slurped at his tea.

'But you're fine. It'll be damn near six o'clock in the morning before we get back. There won't be a soul aboot to worry you.'

✧

Peeny couldn't have been more wrong. They were halfway along the loch when they saw activity on the piers. The closer they came to the harbour, the clearer it became that a large crowd had gathered to welcome the lost mariners home.

'Sandy won't be happy about this,' said Robertson.

'Bugger him,' said Connelly, nursing his nose through a hankie. 'This damn thing will have to be reset. I wonder why there's so many people aboot at this time o' morning? I know Sandy's popular – in some quarters – but the place is hoaching.'

Robertson stayed tight-lipped, avoiding Connelly's gaze.

'Hang on. You didna mention anything aboot that bloody star to Mitchell, did you?'

Robertson inclined his head. 'Och, I might have let it slip a wee bit.'

'In that case, we're for it now.'

'What dae you mean?'

'Christmas miracle, that sort o' thing. You wait, Davie.'

As Robertson came alongside the pier, he could see more than a hundred people huddling in the cold, awaiting their return.

'Sandy!' Peeny shouted below. 'There's a few folk aboot. Davie's just tying her up and we can get going.'

'Is Dreich there?'

Peeny pulled his head from the hatch and scanned the crowd. 'I canna see him.'

'Do me a favour, Peeny. Get Mitchell to give us a hurl back hame in his Rover.'

'I will, don't worry.' He stepped away from the hatch and leaned through the wheelhouse window. 'Sit tight just now. I'm going to cadge a lift for Sandy.'

With the skill born of years at sea, Peeny stepped across the gap between the boat and the pier. The first person to greet him was an eager-looking young man with a notepad and pencil poised.

'I'm Craig MacIntyre from the *Kinloch Herald*.'

'I know. I was at school with your grandfaither. Man, I was at your christening.'

Ignoring this, MacIntyre continued. 'Can you tell us something about your experience with the star that led you to the missing men?'

'Och, there was nothing to it. There it was twinkling away, so we just followed it.'

'The three of you?'

'Aye, the three o' us.'

'This is going to make such a good story.'

'I'm glad you think so. We were doing what we could to save oor friends. Something any decent person should be willing to be aboot.'

'Quickly, can I ask you, what condition were Mr Hoynes and Hamish in when you found them?'

Peeny hesitated. 'It's fair to say they weren't themselves, that's for sure.'

'Distressed, likely?'

'Aye, you could say that as well, right enough.'

'And how did they greet you? Were there tears, hugs?'

'It's fair to say there was some hugging on the go, for sure.

Aye, and a lot o' wailing, into the bargain.' Peeny looked rather discomfited.

'Can you describe the star? Did it appear in the east?'

'It was just there, in the sky. It looked like a star. Och, I'll need to go, son. And before you ask, I never saw Balthazar at his feast neither.'

The young reporter watched Peeny hurry off. Everybody needed a break when they were starting out on a career. A star. Christmas. A rescue against the odds. Craig MacIntyre's break was surely here and now. He ran back up the pier, anxious to get to work on the story of a lifetime. But the story about the appearance in the sky of a Russian satellite in last week's edition suddenly dawned on him. MacIntyre felt his chance of fame slipping away. But he considered his story so sensational, he resolved to go ahead anyway.

Mitchell the harbour master just wanted the pier cleared of people, so he told Peeny he was happy to offer Hoynes and Hamish a lift home.

'We'll have to force oor way through all these folk, Sandy,' said Hamish.

'I'd happily force my way through the Red Army, so long as Dreich's nowhere to be seen.'

'Definitely no sign o' him at all.'

'Good. Then there's no time like the present,' said Hoynes.

With Peeny taking the lead, Hoynes and Hamish followed, the collars of their pea jackets up round their faces, and bunnets pulled down low, like armour against the throng.

'It's a miracle!' shouted Maureen Gillespie.

'Hoynes is anointed, so he is,' commented Alan Cunningham, using the old Kinloch saying intended for those who enjoyed extraordinary fortune.

'The luck o' the devil, mair like,' said someone anonymous in the crowd.

'Away! They saw a sign – a star!' Jean Monteath, a pious woman and a pillar of the Wee Kirk, was having none of it.

'Damn me,' said Hamish. 'We'll need a miracle to get through this lot.'

Though progress was slow, they soon reached the harbour master's office and were glad to get in out of the crowd.

'Man, that was hectic, and no mistake,' said Hoynes. 'This bloody star nonsense is all they're interested in. We could have frozen to death and it wouldna have mattered. Were the three o' you on the whisky when you saw it?'

'I swear to you, Sandy. It was there – a great big thing, fair twinkling right o'er where yous were – well, where yous were *camping*.' Peeny adopted an innocent expression.

'Can you take us home now, Mitchell? I could sleep for a week – the sleep o' the just, mark you. Aye, and Hamish's mother will be waiting to tuck him in.'

'And Mrs Green the minister's wife, I shouldna wonder,' said Peeny, earning a glare from the *Girl Maggie*'s first mate.

'Follow me,' said Mitchell. 'We can use the back door. Hopefully it'll be quieter.'

They stepped back into the chill, dark morning and headed to Mitchell's Rover, parked beside a stumpy metal bollard.

Hoynes was about to open the car door when he felt a tap on his shoulder.

'Let me get in this bloody thing, will you, Hamish? Time is of the essence.' Hoynes turned, ready to berate the younger man. But it wasn't Hamish who was picked out in the lamplight. Dreich MacCallum stood tall, his gaunt frame draped in an expensive overcoat.

'Have you been away on a wee holiday, Sandy?' said Dreich, his signature sickly smile spread across his face.

'I was off on business, as well you know.'

Dreich snorted a dismissive laugh. 'What kind of business is to be done in a tent camped at Portroy? It sounds to me as though you were on the run.'

'Run fae you, Dreich MacCallum? There'll be green snow and yellow hailstones the day that happens, for sure.' Hoynes stared back at his tormentor, gimlet-eyed.

'I have news for you, Sandy. You'll not have forgotten you sank my cabin cruiser with your reckless behaviour?'

'Not true – it was an engine malfunction.'

'Not in my lawyer's opinion. He's here in Kinloch, you know. We're suing for compensation. I know you don't have the money. But I'm a fair man, and I want to give you a chance to redeem yourself.'

'I've nothing to redeem myself for, Dreich.'

'Under the circumstances, I think I'd prefer *Mr MacCallum*. But it's a simple choice. You're all here to bear witness to my extremely generous offer.' He turned to face Hamish, Peeny and Mitchell.

'We'll need to hear it before we decide how generous it is, Dreich,' said Peeny.

'Extremely so, I'd say. Perhaps too generous – certainly more than this old rascal deserves.'

'Och, just spit it oot,' said Hamish.

'It's time to put an old story to bed. I'll race you to the buoy at the head of the loch. Just the two of us in rowing boats – like back in the old days. If you win, I'll walk away, Sandy. I'm a rich man, and I daresay the insurance will cover part of the cost of my boat, if not all.'

'And if I lose?'

'I take possession of the *Girl Maggie*. Outright, you understand. No half-share or employing you to do the fishing. I'll have her and do what I want with the tub. Just think, she'd make a fine display at Hogmanay, burning out in the loch, the way the Vikings used to do, eh?'

A pool of light from the lamppost held them motionless: five men from the same wee town, the air heavy with tension. They seemed frozen in time, a tableau vivant at the end of the pier.

'You're on!' said Hoynes. He spat on his meaty right hand, Dreich did the same, and they shook on the agreement.

'How about Christmas Eve? As good a day as any, and the forecast is fair. It'll be cold, but the loch will be like a millpond, Sandy.'

Hoynes gave a curt incline of the head. Saying no more, he turned and ducked into Mitchell's Rover.

23

The few days leading up to Christmas Eve were charged with excitement in Kinloch. Some thought the whole thing foolhardy. Others reckoned it to be nothing but a stunt and swore that Hoynes was set to gain financially, somehow. After all, his track record of coming up smelling of roses was so long as to have achieved legendary status.

However, those closest to the skipper of the *Girl Maggie* wrung their hands and fretted over the whole arrangement. Marjorie pleaded with her husband not to be so foolish. After all, he was no longer an energetic teenager, and the price of failure was high.

Hamish wondered when Hoynes had last rowed any real distance. His memory was full of awkward attempts to manoeuvre their little tender back to the *Girl Maggie* in places like Lochranza or Gairsay. He told himself that Hoynes would at least be sober on this occasion, though he was by no means mollified by the thought.

Not only did Hoynes stand to lose his fishing boat, but they would also lose their employment. Though the first mate didn't give it voice, he thought the whole arbitrary notion of it all rather selfish. Hoynes was nearing retirement and would have a pension to meet his needs. Hamish had no such luxury.

The subject was also a hot one round the bar of the County Hotel. To such an extent, in fact, that a book had been opened on the race. Though Hoynes was a friend to almost every customer, the betting was heavily against him. Especially so when Dreich was spotted ploughing up and down the loch in a sleek rowing boat he'd borrowed from the boatbuilder in Tarbert. He was getting himself in shape for the contest.

But Hoynes was intractable on the subject. Not only did he refuse to put in any practice prior to the race, he hadn't even sourced a suitable craft in which to participate. No matter how Hamish, Peeny, Connelly and the rest tried to coax him, he adopted a studiously laissez-faire attitude to the whole thing, happily indulging in drams and pre-festive fare in abundance. The suggestion that he might be advised to put in some time on the oars was greeted with a puff of tobacco smoke and a raised brow.

To put it mildly, those closest to Hoynes considered that he'd temporarily lost his mind. Hamish was more inclined to think that the condition was of a permanent nature and found himself leafing through the Situations Vacant page of the *Kinloch Herald*, especially after the latest edition of the paper appeared, complete with a mocked-up star on the front page.

But inexorably, the fateful day dawned. As Dreich had predicted, Christmas Eve did so dry and cold with little more than a light breeze to ripple the still waters of the loch.

That Hoynes had asked to use Davie Robertson's tender as his weapon of choice in the upcoming contest did little to discourage those betting against him. Though a sizeable wager laid by Margaret Patterson – a kind woman who always supported the underdog – in Hoynes's favour did raise an eyebrow or two, it did very little to alter the odds: Dreich MacCallum remained the overwhelming favourite.

As they had so many years before, a large crowd gathered at Kinloch harbour, ready to see the contestants battle it out. Though the weather was bitter, Pallini's ice-cream van was doing a roaring trade in crisps, confectionery and cigarettes, while George's fish-and-chip van sold everything from pies, haggis, tea and, of course, its eponymous wares. Children ran about, energised by chocolate and Christmas, while the older townsfolk cast a leery eye over the adversaries. Such was the level of anticipation and excitement, the bar staff at the County Hotel had been allowed to close, to witness this spectacle at first hand, for as long as the contest endured. In any event, the bar would have been empty as Sandy Hoynes and Dreich MacCallum slogged it out.

Dreich was the first to appear. He strode out of a rented motor car in a bright blue tracksuit, white plimsolls and a brightly coloured scarf, in the colours of the shipping line for whom he captained – or so it was said.

As those assembled awaited Hoynes's appearance, critical eyes were cast over the boats to be used in the race. The Tarbert rowing boat to be occupied by Dreich was freshly varnished and looked as sleek as a birlinn. Beside it, the *Sea Harvester* appeared short, squat and poorly turned out. But, still, there was a race to be won and sport to be had.

When Hoynes appeared, he did so in a surprising fashion, coming straight off the midday bus from the scheme. As he forced his way through the spectators, it was clear he'd made very little effort to dress appropriately for a sporting contest and he looked very much the same as he normally did. His one concession was the abandonment of his oilskin, so he was stripped down to his usual moleskin trousers and fisherman's jumper – though he had refused to part with his sou'wester that was aligned fore and aft to aid wind resistance.

'You'll be turning oot for the Oxford Boat Race next,' shouted one wag. But Hoynes ignored that and every other taunt, as he stood beside Dreich at the top of the sea-stairs awaiting the harbour master. Mitchell had been deputised as starter and umpire, and his decision on any foul play or incident would be final and indisputable. An arrangement agreed upon by both participants.

Hoynes cast his eyes to the New Quay, where the *Girl Maggie* still sat on Galbraith's slip. Some said there was a tear in his eye, others that it was merely an effect of the cold weather. The speculation was soon halted when the door to the harbour master's office was seen to swing open, and Mitchell made his way up the pier to a ragged cheer.

On arrival, he put his whistle to his mouth and issued forth one long blast, hushing the chatter of the crowd.

'When this next sounds, you must make your way to your boats and commence the race. Is that understood?'

Dreich, jogging on the spot, nodded enthusiastically, while Hoynes merely inclined his head.

'I want a fair contest, as befits the gentlemen concerned.'

That induced much hilarity, which Mitchell ignored.

'Mr Hoynes, Mr MacCallum, please take your positions at the top of the stairs.'

Dreich dashed to his spot, adopting the stance of a sprinter waiting for the gun, while Hoynes ambled into position, hands in pockets.

Again, Mitchell put the whistle to his mouth, but he was

momentarily distracted by the appearance of Donnie in the ambulance. The local doctors were of the collective opinion that while Dreich MacCallum looked in good shape, Hoynes gave the impression of a coronary waiting to happen. And to this end, the lifeboat was standing at anchor in the loch, ready to assist any participant in difficulty.

Composing himself once more, Mitchell put the whistle to his lips and blew.

Dreich pelted down the steps and was soon in his rowing boat. He pushed himself off the harbour wall with gusto and was quickly into his stride, vigorous strokes propelling the boat out of the harbour.

Still looking unruffled, Hoynes eased himself into the little rowing boat, angled it off the wall with a feeble push and set about the oars as though he was embarking upon a leisurely plooter across to the New Quay.

Marjorie, standing beside Hamish, hid her head behind his arm. 'Please tell me he's putting more effort into it.'

Hamish grimaced as the distance between Hoynes and Dreich stretched. 'Just you keep your heid roon there, Mrs Hoynes. Come on, Sandy!' he shouted, hoping his cries might engender a spirit of competition in his skipper. But Hoynes was into a regular, if somewhat pedestrian stroke pattern. There seemed to be little effort behind his rowing, though he had pushed his sou'wester to the back of his head as, perhaps, an indication of determination.

The crowd roared, cheered, laughed and booed by turns, as Dreich MacCallum turned round mid-stroke to see how his competitor was faring. He shook his head and aimed a sarcastic wave at Hoynes rowing oh-so-steadily behind.

'What on earth does Sandy think he's doing?' said Peeny,

standing in a small group of fishermen. 'Man, he's making a laughing stock o' himself. No effort whatsoever.'

'That's the *Girl Maggie* a goner,' said Connelly. 'We should have left him in the tent.'

The crowd were becoming restive, too. They'd come to enjoy a spirited race to the finish: before them was a drubbing – no contest, a farce.

'Too much booze, Hoynes!' shouted Derek Kelly. 'You're paying the price now!' He and the skipper had a poor relationship since Hoynes had accidentally fallen onto his car bonnet after a particularly refreshing night in the County Hotel. Though the fisherman had paid for the broken wing mirror, the animus between them continued.

Both contestants were out in the loch now, though Dreich was forging ahead. Hoynes, on the other hand, maintained his unfaltering pace, pulling the boat forward but losing ground by the second.

'What's happening, Hamish?' said Marjorie, her head still tucked behind his back.

'You'll no' like it, Mrs H. Dreich's fair pushing on, and Sandy's just oot for a dander.'

Marjorie let out a muffled wail. 'I knew this would happen. He'd been too jocose about it all. Had a few drams by the fire last night as though nothing was happening. He's just given up.'

Hamish had to agree. Though he'd never expected Hoynes to win the race, he'd hoped his skipper would at least try.

Then, something happened that sent a gasp of disbelief through the crowd. Hoynes stowed his oars, delved into his pocket and produced his pipe, which he proceeded to tamp down as though he'd not a care in the world. He set light to it and puffed away contentedly, as Dreich disappeared up the loch.

There were howls of derision from the crowd, and some spectators began to drift away. All were disappointed that this pre-festive spectacle had turned into a damp squib.

'What on earth's happening now, Hamish?'

'Well, Sandy's having a wee breather, as far as I can tell.'

'What?' Marjorie whipped her head from behind Hamish's back and gaped at her husband as he placed the oars back in the blue waters of the loch and, with pipe clenched between his teeth, resumed his stately progress.

Unseen by many spectators, a venerable black Bentley turned off the roundabout and made its way down the pier. If anyone had been looking, they'd have seen Campbell the lawyer step out of the car, puffing on his cigar. He made his way towards Mitchell, the pair exchanged a few words, then the harbour master reached for his whistle and blew one long, shrill blast.

Out on the loch, near enough to hear it, Hoynes turned round. He saw the distant figure of Mitchell waving in a beckoning motion. Hoynes took a long puff of his pipe, turned the boat round by use of one oar, and headed back to the Old Quay. Dreich, well out of earshot of the whistle, ploughed on, racing for the buoy which marked the turning point and the halfway marker in the race.

Hamish and Marjorie couldn't believe what they were seeing. Though they weren't sure why Mitchell had blown his whistle, the fact that Hoynes was now rowing in the wrong direction left them open-mouthed.

Marjorie moaned.

'I'll take a wee wander doon the pier, Mrs H, and see if I can find out what's going on,' said Hamish.

By the time Hoynes had tied up his craft at the far end of the pier and ascended the ladder there, Dreich had navigated the buoy and was on his way back to finish the race. Mitchell, Campbell and Hoynes waited for him at the end of the pier.

Before Dreich was in the harbour, another car drove down the Old Quay. It pulled up beside Campbell's Bentley, and a man in a trilby hat and raincoat exited the vehicle.

Hamish, who'd remained an observer until now, thought it time to have a word with his skipper. He made his way over to Hoynes, who was enjoying a quiet puff of his pipe atop a bollard.

'What on earth is happening, Sandy?'

'The victory of light o'er darkness, Hamish. A wrong righted after many years.'

Still none the wiser, Hamish looked on as Dreich crossed the notional finishing line between the twin piers. Soaked in sweat, despite the chill of the day, he raised his arms in triumph, though looked puzzled to see Hoynes sitting calmly on the bollard with his pipe.

Mitchell put a loudhailer to his mouth. 'Come in, Mr MacCallum. I've people here who want to speak to you.'

Dreich secured his boat beside Sandy's and climbed the ladder to the pier.

'You're finished, Hoynes! You'll hand me the ownership papers to your boat at your earliest convenience.' He laughed, eyeing those present.

It was Campbell the lawyer's turn to speak. 'I wouldn't be so sure about that, Mr MacCallum. Some irregularities have come to light.'

'What?'

'Such as: the company who fabricated the part of Mr

Hoynes's engine that subsequently sunk your cabin cruiser has admitted liability. But, as it turns out, the vessel wasn't seaworthy in the first place. Aye, and you knew it, too.' Campbell turned to the man in the trilby.

'My name is Inspector Black from the Glasgow Police, Mr MacCallum. I'm here to place you under arrest.'

'I'm sorry, what are you talking about, inspector?' said Dreich.

'Your cabin cruiser was taken into dry dock in Glasgow in November, is that right?'

'Yes, what of it?' Dreich's manner was still defiant, but a shadow had crossed his face.

'The yard told you that there were major structural problems with the vessel that would take some thousands of pounds to correct.' Black consulted his notebook. 'Undeterred by this, you sold the craft to a Mr Simon McGeady in Oban. I believe he was to take delivery of her on January the sixth.'

'Yes, but what's that got to do with you?'

'The boat was dangerous, not seaworthy. You were told to take her out of the water in Glasgow. You have no insurance, and you misrepresented its condition to Mr McGeady. There's a lot to talk about here, Mr MacCallum, so I'd be grateful if you'd accompany me to Kinloch Police Station. This way, please, sir.' Inspector Black caught Dreich's wrist and began to pull him away.

'But I still won the race fair and square. It was a wager agreed upon by gentlemen. The *Girl Maggie* is mine!'

'I had to terminate the contest, Dreich,' said Mitchell. 'It's now null and void.'

Dreich MacCallum glared at Hoynes. 'You think you've

won, Sandy, but you're wrong. Wait until my solicitor sorts this out. You'll see!'

'If you're talking about Mr Fincher, he's gone back to London,' said Campbell. 'Turns out that you owe him money – a great deal of money. When he heard my tale about your losing your job, and your attempt to defraud Mr McGeady, well, he thought it best to cut his losses. And I believe your wife returned to London with him.'

Dreich MacCallum was still ranting as he was escorted to the police car.

Hoynes put another match to his pipe. 'You see, Hamish, there's nothing to be gained by dishonesty, right enough. Let that be a lesson for the rest o' your life. Always be an honest man. It's the only way.'

Hamish, Campbell and Mitchell looked at Hoynes, each man lost in his own thoughts.

Epilogue

Some years later...

The old man cursed as he pushed his foot down on the accelerator. He coughed weakly as the elderly Austin Cambridge chugged up the hill, then followed the winding road down towards a forest of stout pine trees, the blue sea of the sound sparkling beyond.

He parked the car on a verge and patted the steering wheel.

'Goodbye, old friend,' he said, a tear meandering down his hollow cheeks into his sparse beard.

He made heavy work of exiting the car, pausing to pull up his trousers, which hung from braces over his wasted frame. The illness that had haunted his last two years was winning the race, and its end was near.

The old man made his way to a wooden gate, pushed it open, and wandered down a grassy path towards the sea. He stopped, leaning on the two sticks he'd brought to ease his passage. Sniffing the air, he could smell rain on the way. He turned on his heel, taking in his surroundings. The heather on the hills, the green grass where cattle grazed peacefully, the trees, the sky in which a large gull soared: all were precious to him. He could hardly bear the thought he'd never see them again.

The distance to the rocky beach was short – a hundred yards at most. But by the time he felt the sea breeze on his face, he was breathing so hard that he was forced to take a seat on a rock, ready for one last effort.

As he gazed out to sea, watching its colour change in the fading light of the gloaming, many faces crossed his mind's eye. He remembered a cold, snowy night in a tent, and again had to wipe away a tear.

Having caught his breath, the old man forced himself up and shuffled along the sand to the water's edge. He took a deep draw of the salt air into his lungs and began to cough once more. The great gull circled overhead, its plaintive cry echoing from the hills beyond.

'Aye, it's all been grand,' he said, stepping into the gentle waves.

He waded out, the ocean supporting his weight like a lover. The time for tears was over.

At first, he saw the flames at her prow. Then he heard the chatter of the men as they rowed towards him.

'Sandy! It's time, my friend.' The Viking, dressed in shining leather, his long blond hair pulled back into a ponytail, leaned a foot on the low gunwale.

'I hate to say goodbye, Hona.'

'There is no such thing as goodbye, Sandy Hoynes. Your spirit will live forever with mine and those who you've loved and lost.' The big Norseman held out a hand and pulled the dying fisherman aboard the sleek longship.

The Sandy Hoynes who stepped onto its deck was wrought anew. Gone was the pain, the struggle for breath, the dread in his heart. He stood tall and strong, his fair hair shining in the low sun, as the longship made for the open sea.

The DCI Daley thriller series

Book 1: *Whisky from Small Glasses*
DCI Jim Daley is sent from the city to investigate a murder after the body of a woman is washed up on an idyllic beach on the west coast of Scotland. Far away from urban resources, he finds himself a stranger in a close-knit community.

Book 2: *The Last Witness*
James Machie was a man with a genius for violence, his criminal empire spreading beyond Glasgow into the UK and mainland Europe. Fortunately, Machie is dead, assassinated in the back of a prison ambulance following his trial and conviction. But now, five years later, he is apparently back from the grave, set on avenging himself on those who brought him down.

Book 3: *Dark Suits and Sad Songs*
When a senior Edinburgh civil servant spectacularly takes his own life in Kinloch harbour, DCI Jim Daley comes face to face with the murky world of politics. To add to his woes, two local drug dealers lie dead, ritually assassinated. It's clear that dark forces are at work in the town.

Book 4: *The Rat Stone Serenade*
It's December, and the Shannon family are heading to their clifftop mansion near Kinloch for their AGM. Shannon International, one

of the world's biggest private companies, has brought untold wealth and privilege to the family. However, a century ago, Archibald Shannon stole the land upon which he built their home – and his descendants have been cursed ever since.

Book 5: *The Well of the Winds*
As World War Two nears its end, a man is stabbed to death on the Kinloch shoreline, in the shadow of the great warships in the harbour. When DCI Daley comes into possession of a journal written by his wartime predecessor in Kinloch, he soon realises that he must solve a murder from the past to uncover the shocking events of the present.

Book 6: *The Relentless Tide*
When Professor Francombe and her team of archaeologists find the remains of three women on a remote Kintyre hillside – a site rumoured to have been the base of Viking warlord Somerled – their delight soon turns to horror when they realise the women tragically met their end only two decades ago.

It soon becomes clear that these are the three missing victims of the 'Midweek Murderer', a serial killer who was at work in Glasgow in the early 1990s. DCI Jim Daley now has the chance to put things right – to confront a nightmare from his past and solve a crime he failed to as a young detective.

Book 7: *A Breath on Dying Embers*
When the luxury cruiser *Great Britain* berths in Kinloch harbour, the pressure mounts on DCI Jim Daley. The high-powered international delegates on board are touring the country, golfing and sightseeing, as part of a UK government trade mission. But within hours, one of the crew members vanishes and a local birdwatcher has disappeared.

Book 8: *Jeremiah's Bell*

Teenager Alison Doig disappeared from Kinloch over thirty years ago under mysterious circumstances. Her reclusive family still live in a remote part of the Kintyre peninsula, amidst rumours of wrecking, smuggling and barbaric cruelty.

Now rich American hotelier Alice Wenger has arrived in town, determined to punish those who made her suffer in the past. But someone has vowed to keep hidden sins concealed for ever.

Book 9: *For Any Other Truth*

When a light aircraft crash-lands at Machrie airport, DCI Jim Daley and his colleague Brian Scott rush to the scene. But it soon becomes clear that both occupants of the plane were dead before take-off.

Meanwhile in Kinloch, local fisherman Hamish is unwittingly dragged into danger when he witnesses something he shouldn't have, and hotel manager Annie is beginning to suspect her new boss may not be as he first appeared. And just as Chief Superintendent Carrie Symington thinks she has finally escaped the sins of her past, she finds herself caught in an even deadlier trap.

As the action spills across the sea to County Antrim – all under the scrutiny of the Security Service – the search is on for any other truth.

Book 10: *The Death of Remembrance*

Glasgow, 1983, and a beat constable walks away from a bar where he knows a crime is about to be committed. It is a decision that will haunt him for the rest of his life.

In the present, a fisherman is found dead by Kinloch's shoreline and a stranger with a deadly mission moves into town.

Meanwhile, DCI Jim Daley must confront old friends, new foes and ghosts who will not be silenced.

Short Stories and Tales from Kinloch

One Last Dram Before Midnight: The Complete Collected DCI Daley Short Stories

Published together for the first time in one not-to-be-missed volume are all Denzil Meyrick's short stories. Discover how DCI Daley and DS Scott first met on the mean streets of Glasgow in two prequels that shed light on their earlier lives. Join Hamish and his old mentor, skipper Sandy Hoynes, as they become embroiled with some Russian fishermen and an illicit whisky plot. And in present-day Kinloch Daley and Scott investigate ghosts from the past, search for a silent missing man, and follow the trail of an elusive historical necklace.

Dalintober Moon: A DCI Daley Story

When a body is found in a whisky barrel buried on Dalintober beach, it appears that a notorious local crime, committed over a century ago, has finally been solved. However, the legacy of murder still resonates within the community, and the tortured screams of a man who died long ago still echo across Kinloch.

Two One Three: A Constable Jim Daley Short Story

Glasgow, 1986. Only a few months into his new job, Constable Jim Daley is pounding the beat. When he is seconded to the CID to help catch a possible serial killer, he makes a new friend, DC Brian Scott. Jim Daley tackles his first serious crime in an investigation that will change his life for ever.

Empty Nets and Promises

It's July 1968, and fishing-boat skipper Sandy Hoynes has his daughter's wedding to pay for – but where are all the fish? He and the crew of the *Girl Maggie* come to the conclusion that a newfangled supersonic jet which is being tested in the skies over Kinloch is scaring off the herring.

First mate Hamish comes up with a cunning plan. But they will have to face down a vindictive fishery officer, a suspicious exciseman and the local police sergeant – not to mention a ghostly piper and some Russians.

Single End: A DC Daley Short Story
It's 1989, and Jim Daley is now a fully fledged detective constable. When ruthless gangster James Machie's accountant is found stabbed to death in a multi-storey car park, it's clear all is not well within Machie's organisation. Meanwhile DC Brian Scott must revisit his past in an attempt to uncover the identity of a corrupt police officer.

A Large Measure of Snow: A Tale from Kinloch
It's December 1967, and the town of Kinloch is cut off by heavy snow. The only way to feed and water the townsfolk is for the fishing fleet to sail to Girvan for much-needed supplies. But the skipper of the *Girl Maggie*, Sandy Hoynes, has a problem. First mate Hamish has, to everyone's astonishment, been chosen as Young Fisherman of the Year by a Glasgow newspaper. Marooned in the town and with one eye on a scoop, their reporter decides to join the fishing crew on their mercy mission.

As the blizzards worsen, the crew of the *Girl Maggie* embarks upon a trip like no other, encountering ghostly Vikings, gigantic crustaceans and a helpful seagull.

A Toast to the Old Stones: A Tale from Kinloch
It's 1968, and the fishermen of Kinloch are preparing to celebrate the old New Year on the twelfth of January. The annual pilgrimage to the Auld Stones is a tradition that goes back beyond memory,

and young Hamish, first mate on the *Girl Maggie*, is chuffed that he's been invited to this exclusive gathering.

Meanwhile, it appears that the new owners of the Firdale Hotel are intent upon turning their customers teetotal, such is the exorbitant price they are charging for whisky. Wily skipper Sandy Hoynes comes up with a plan to deliver the spirit to the thirsty villagers at a price they can afford through his connections with a local still-man.

But when the Revenue are tipped off, it looks as though Hoynes and Hamish's mercy mission might run aground. Can the power of the Auld Stones come to their rescue, and is the reappearance of a face from Hoynes' past a sign for good or ill?

For up-to-the-minute news
and information about
Denzil Meyrick's books
and projects find him here

f DenzilMeyrickAuthor

🐦 LochLomonden